I can COLOR Everything!

Written by Tom Donegan
Illustrated by Bess Harding

First published by Parragon in 2012

Parragon
Queen Street House
4 Queen Street
Bath BA1 1HE, UK

ISBN 978-1-4454-6938-6
Printed in the USA

Dinosaurs and prehistoric creatures

Irritator

Irritator had jaws like a crocodile.

Tyrannosaurus rex

Diplodocus

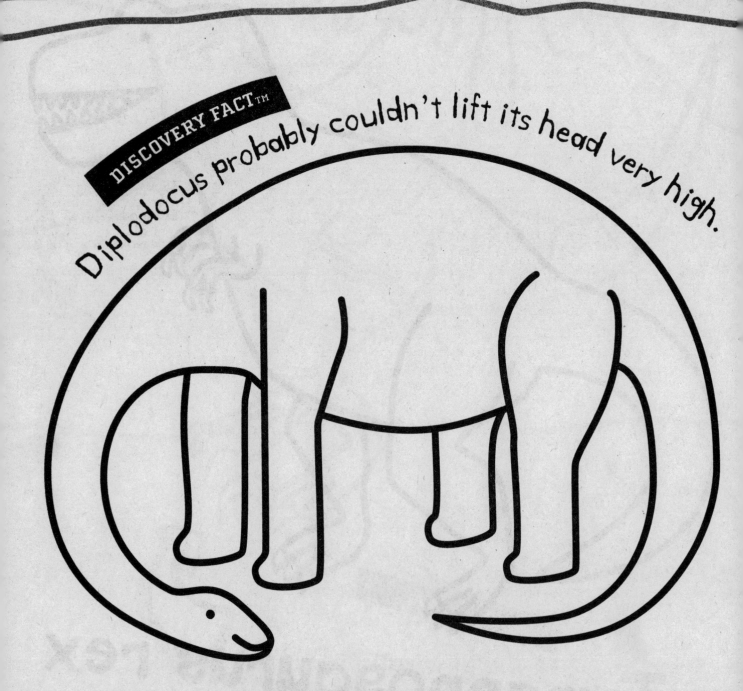

DISCOVERY FACT™

Diplodocus probably couldn't lift its head very high.

Velociraptor

Velociraptor had a
long, sharp toe claw.

DISCOVERY FACT™

This big, chunky animal only ate plants.

Pareiasaurus

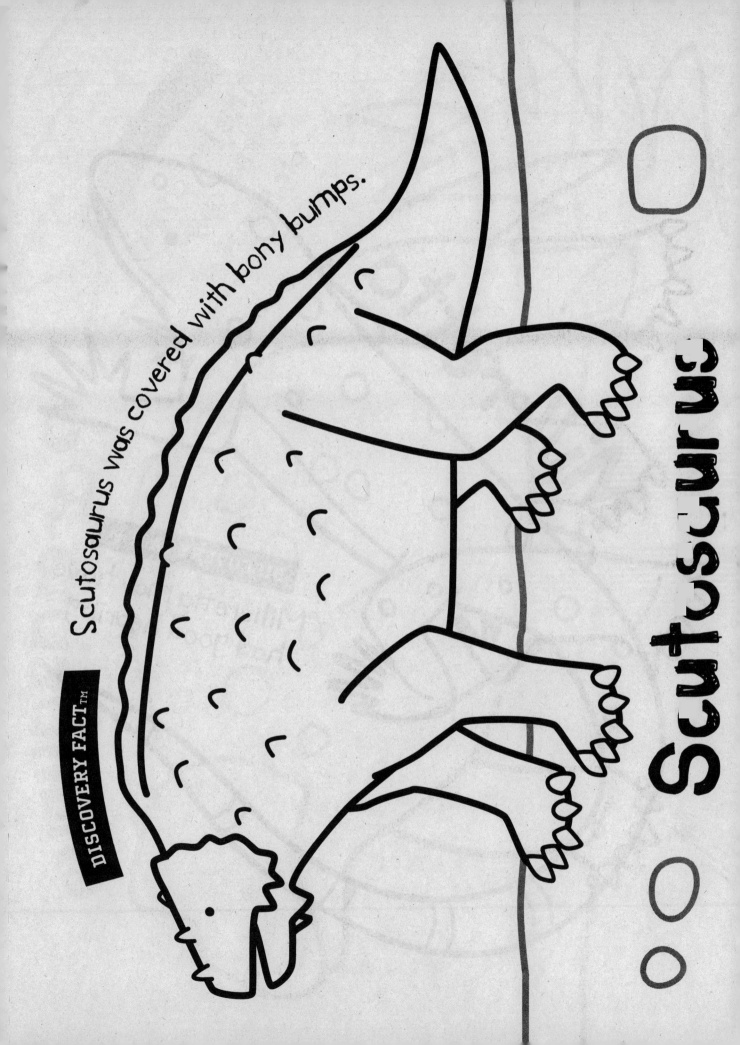

Scutosaurus was covered with bony bumps.

DISCOVERY FACT™

Scutosaurus

Milleretta

DISCOVERY FACT™

Milleretta may have had good hearing.

DISCOVERY FACT™

Paleothyris had sharp teeth for grabbing its prey.

Paleothyris

Eoraptor

Eoraptor moved quickly on its thin back legs.

Albertosaurus

Albertosaurus may have lived together in groups.

Spinosaurus had a huge sail on its back.

Spinosaurus

Acanthostega

DISCOVERY FACT™

Acanthostega had a tail like a fish.

Westlothiana
ate spiders
and insects.
DISCOVERY FACT™

Westlothiana

Ornithomimus

DISCOVERY FACT™

Ornithomimus had a long, thin neck like an ostrich.

DISCOVERY FACT™

Plateosaurus may have stood on its back legs to reach higher leaves.

Plateosaurus

DISCOVERY FACT™

Paradapedon had a strong beak at the front of its jaws.

Paradapedon

Polacanthus

Polacanthus was covered in spikes.

Apatosaurus

DISCOVERY FACT™

Apatosaurus had a very long neck and tail.

Titanosaurus

DISCOVERY FACT™

Titanosaurus swallowed stones to help grind down its food.

Maiasaura

Maiasaura mothers took very good care of their young.

Stegosaurus had
fierce spikes
on its tail.

Stegosaurus

Kentrosaurus

Kentrosaurus had two rows of bony plates and spines on its back.

Saurolophus

This dinosaur had a long, bony spike on the back of its head.

DISCOVERY FACT™

This dinosaur had a long, hollow tube on the back of its head.

Parasaurolophus

Ankylosaurus

DISCOVERY FACT™

Ankylosaurus had short, strong legs.

Triceratops

Triceratops had three horns on its head.

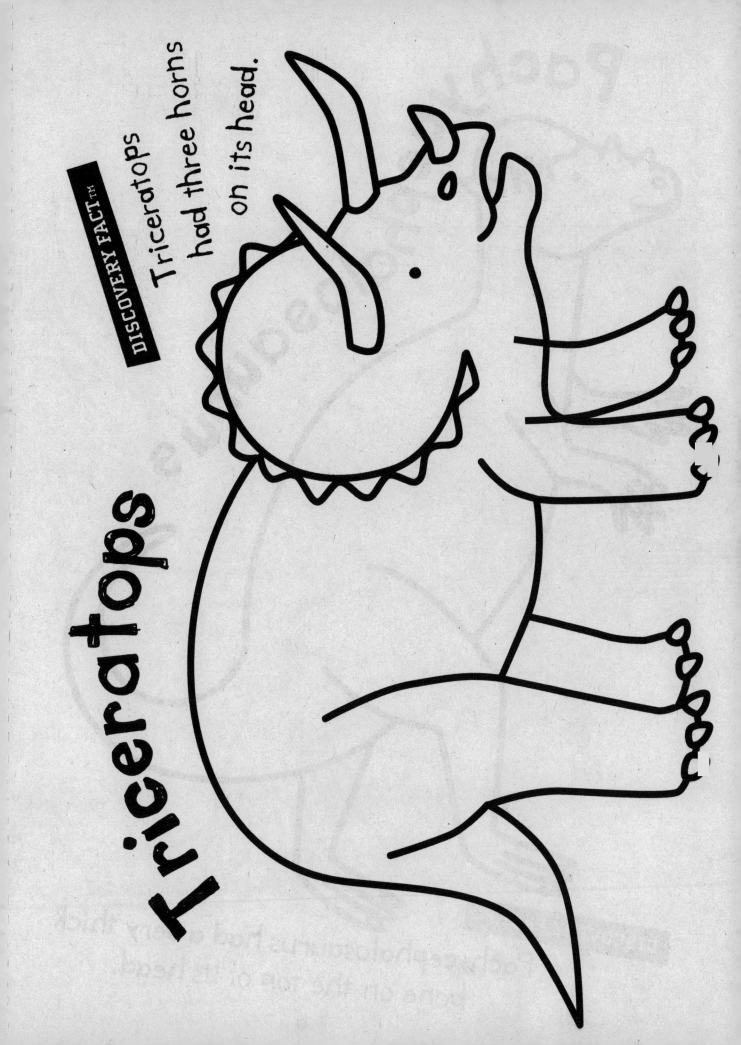

Pachycephalosaurus

DISCOVERY FACT™

Pachycephalosaurus had a very thick bone on the top of its head.

Stygimoloch had spikes all over its face.

Stygimoloch

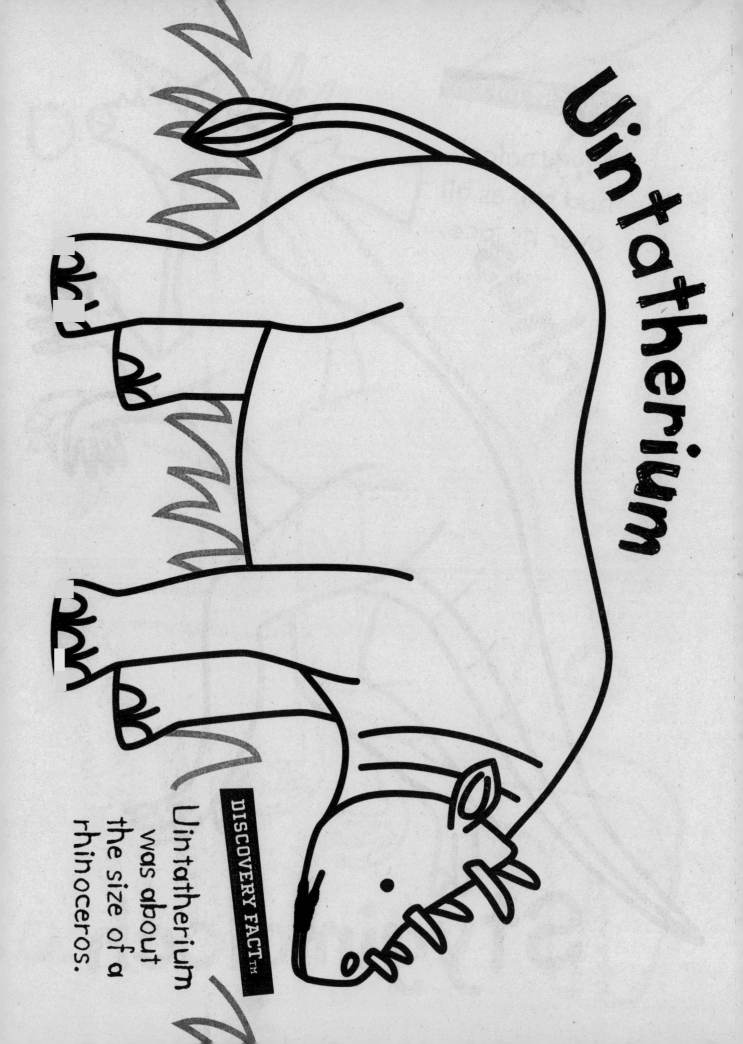

Uintatherium

DISCOVERY FACT™

Uintatherium was about the size of a rhinoceros.

Deinonychus

DISCOVERY FACT™

Deinonychus had sharp, curved claws.

Suchomimus

DISCOVERY FACT™

Suchomimus caught fish with its long snout.

Smilodectes

Smilodectes looked like a lemur.

Eudimorphodon

DISCOVERY FACT™

Eudimorphodon may have used its tail to steer when flying.

Long, narrow wings
helped Pterodactylus
glide through the air.

pterodactylus

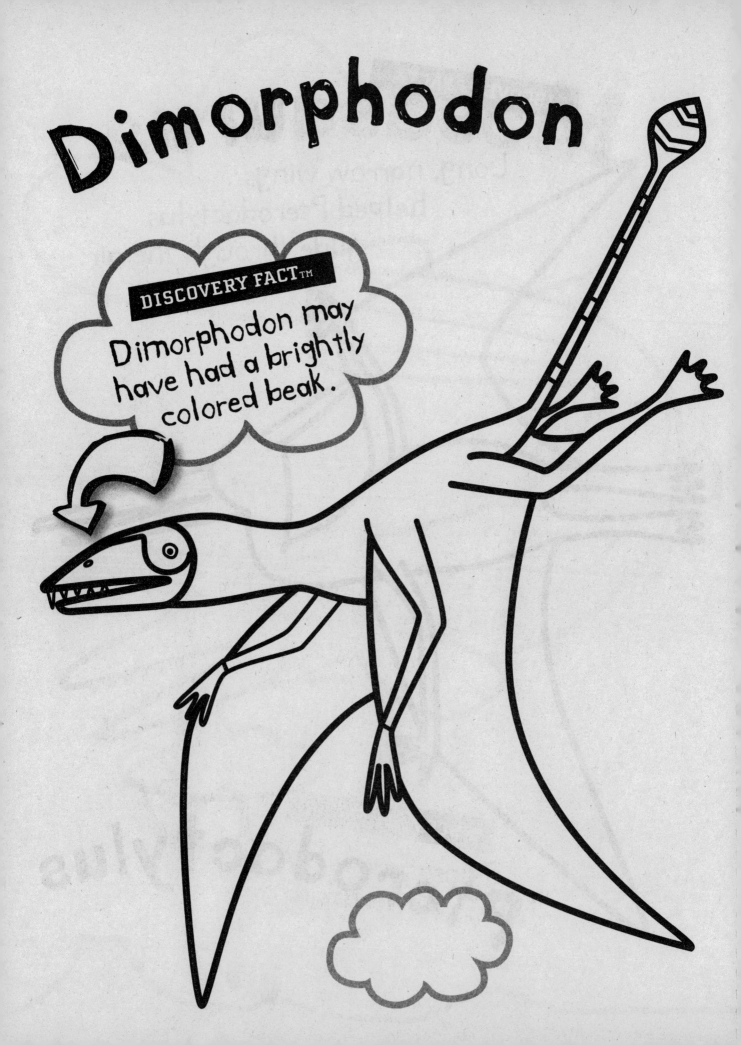

Mosasaurus

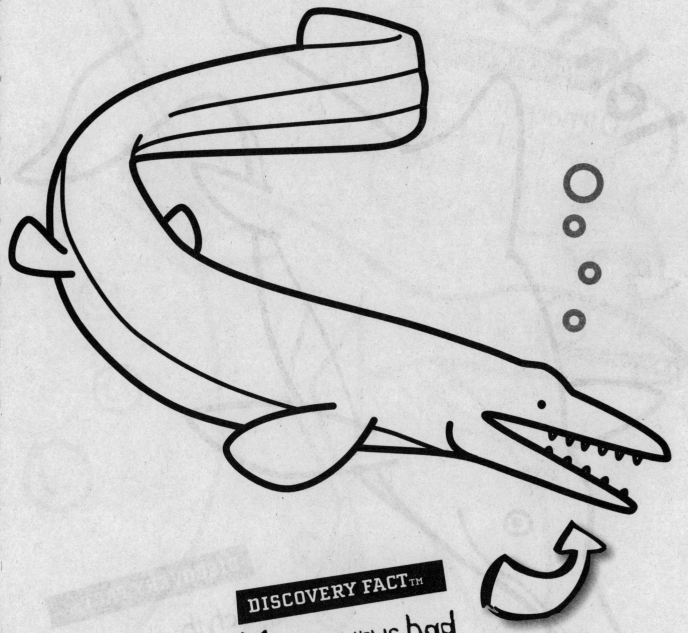

Mosasaurus had very powerful jaws.

Ichthyosaurus

DISCOVERY FACT™

Ichthyosaurus had very big eyes.

Plesiosaurus

DISCOVERY FACT™

This sea creature swam like a turtle with long flippers.

Liopleurodon had a good sense of smell.

Liopleurodon

Shonisaurus

DISCOVERY FACT™

Shonisaurus had a longer body
than Tyrannosaurus rex.

Protostega

Protostega was a
huge turtle.

Henodus

Henodus had a
square-shaped
shell.

Scapanorhynchus

DISCOVERY FACT™

This shark had a long, pointed nose.

DISCOVERY FACT™

Hybodus was a fast-moving hunter.

Hybodus

Tylosaurus

DISCOVERY FACT™

Tylosaurus had a long tail with flaps on the top and bottom.

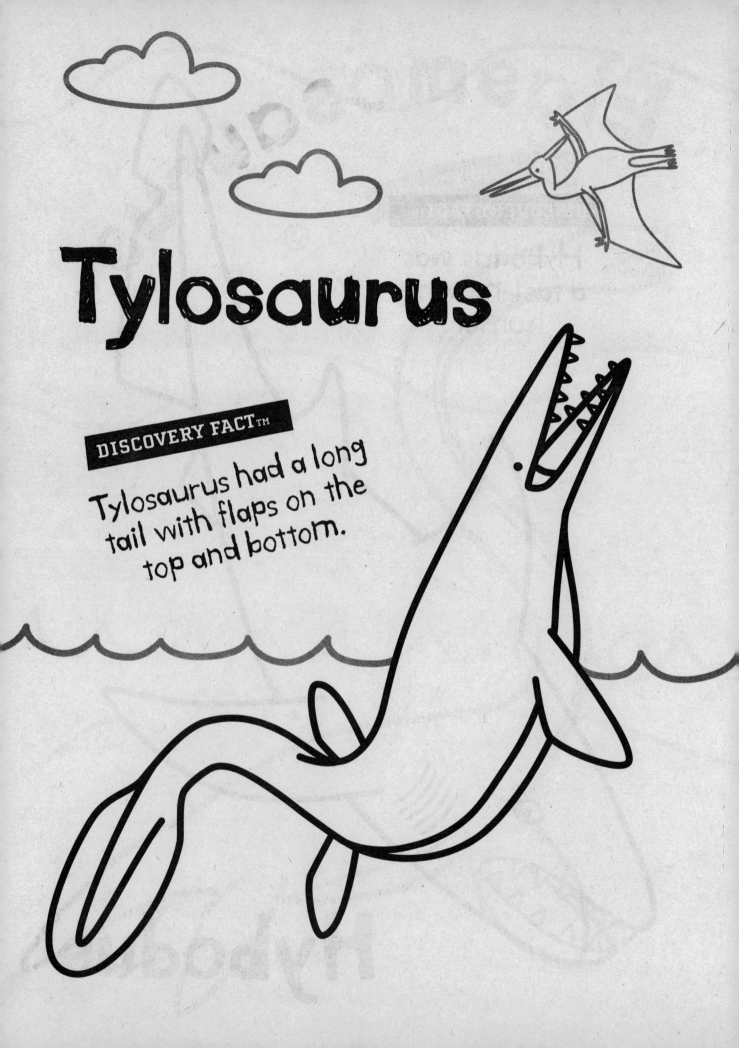

Elasmosaurus

DISCOVERY FACT™

Elasmosaurus had a long, thin neck.

Kronosaurus

DISCOVERY FACT™

Kronosaurus had a huge head filled with big, sharp teeth.

Amazing animals

DISCOVERY FACT™

African elephants never stop growing.

African elephant

Camel

Camels can have either one or two humps.

Bloodhound

Bloodhounds can smell much better than humans.

The red wolf is smaller than the gray wolf.

Red wolf

Chimpanzee

Chimpanzees use stones, sticks, and leaves as tools.

The howler monkey has the loudest call of all the monkeys.

Howler monkey

Chipmunks use their cheek pouches to store food.

Chipmunk

Fennec fox

DISCOVERY FACT™

The fennec fox has big ears that can hear other animals moving underground.

Flying squirrel

DISCOVERY FACT™

Flying squirrels glide from tree to tree, using their tails to steer in the air.

Bat

DISCOVERY FACT™

Bats sleep hanging upside down.

A hippopotamus can
run faster than a man.

Hippopotamus

Kinkajou

DISCOVERY FACT™

The kinkajou uses its long tail as a blanket when sleeping.

Moose

Moose are good swimmers.

The giraffe is the tallest animal in the world.

Giraffe

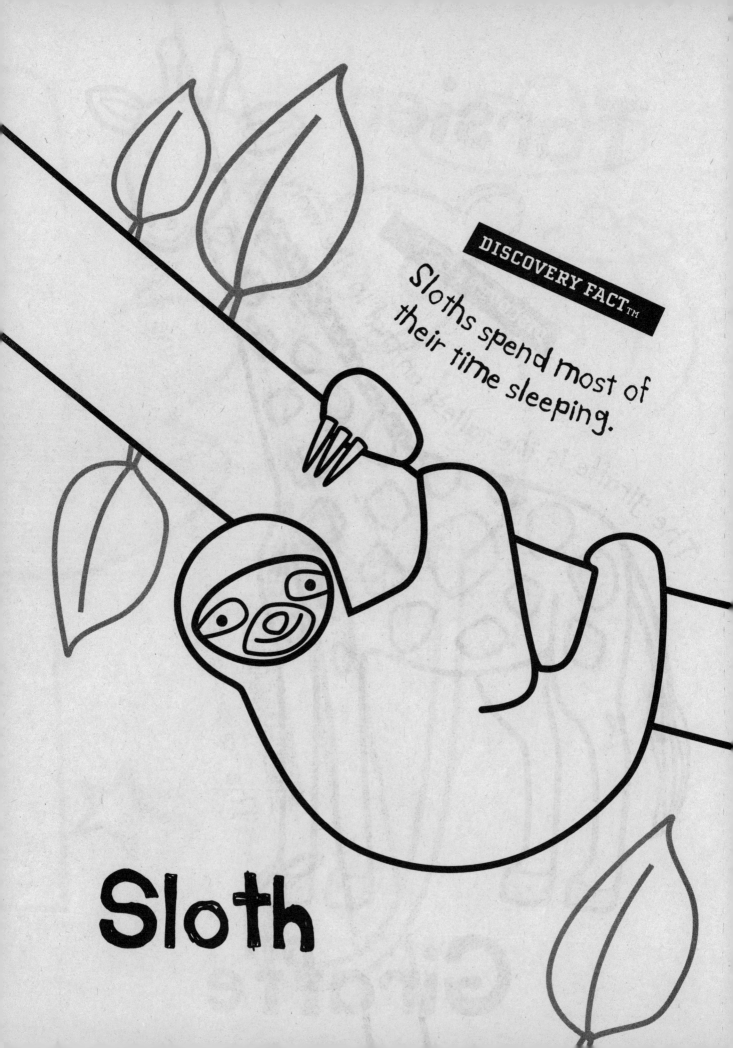

DISCOVERY FACT™

Sloths spend most of their time sleeping.

Sloth

Tarsier

DISCOVERY FACT™

The tarsier's big eyes help it see in the dark.

Kangaroo

Kangaroos are good at jumping, but they cannot run.

Koala

DISCOVERY FACT™

Koalas have fingerprints
just like humans do.

Platypus

DISCOVERY FACT™

The male platypus has a poisonous stinger on its back feet.

Opossum

Opossums carry their babies in a pouch when they are little.

Male birds of paradise show their colorful feathers in a dance.

Bird of paradise

Albatross

The albatross has the biggest wings of any bird.

Flamingo

Flamingos can stand on one leg.

Hummingbird

Hummingbirds can fly backward and upside down.

Ostrich

DISCOVERY FACT™

The ostrich is the tallest and the heaviest bird in the world.

Parrot

DISCOVERY FACT™

Parrots have four toes
on each foot—two point
forward and two point
backward.

Pelican

DISCOVERY FACT™

A pelican uses its large beak to scoop up fish, like a fishing net.

Puffin

DISCOVERY FACT™

Puffins can fly as fast as a car.

Woodpeckers use their strong beaks to dig nest holes in trees.

Woodpecker

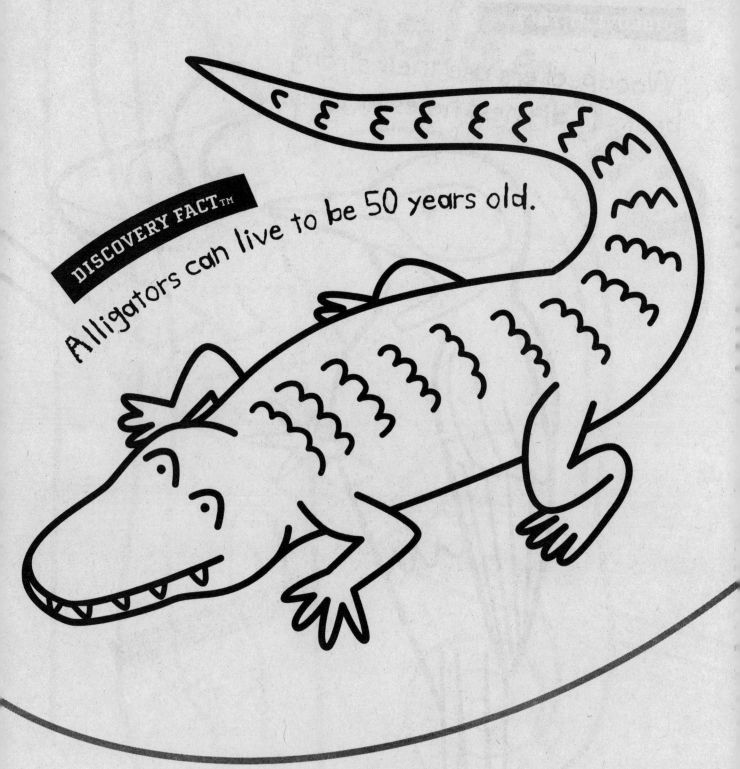

Alligators can live to be 50 years old.

Alligator

Chameleon

A chameleon's tongue can stretch twice the length of its body.

Coconut crab

Coconut crabs use their claws to cut open coconut shells.

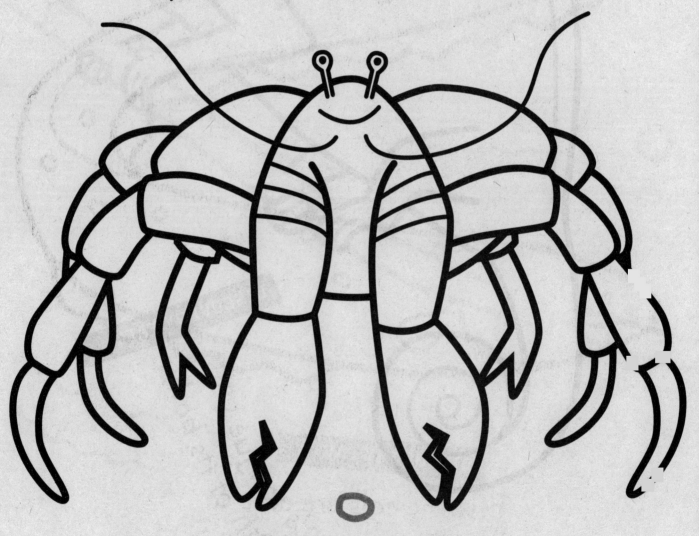

Electric eel

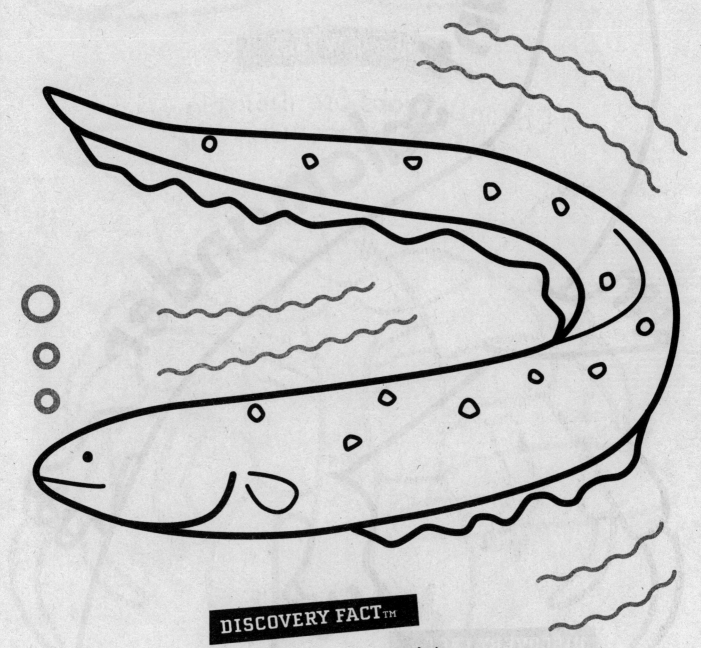

DISCOVERY FACT™

Electric eels are able to make their own electricity.

Giant salamander

DISCOVERY FACT™

The giant salamander is the largest amphibian alive today.

Iguana

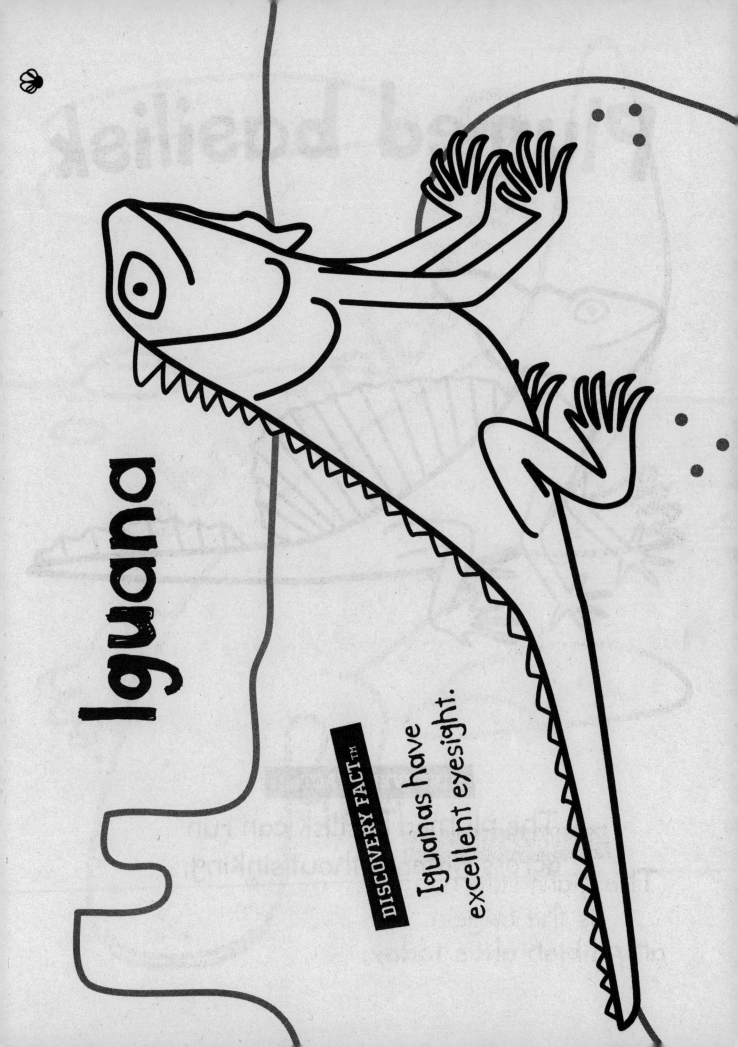

DISCOVERY FACT™

Iguanas have excellent eyesight.

Plumed basilisk

The plumed basilisk can run across water without sinking.

Python

Some pythons can grow to
be longer than two cars.

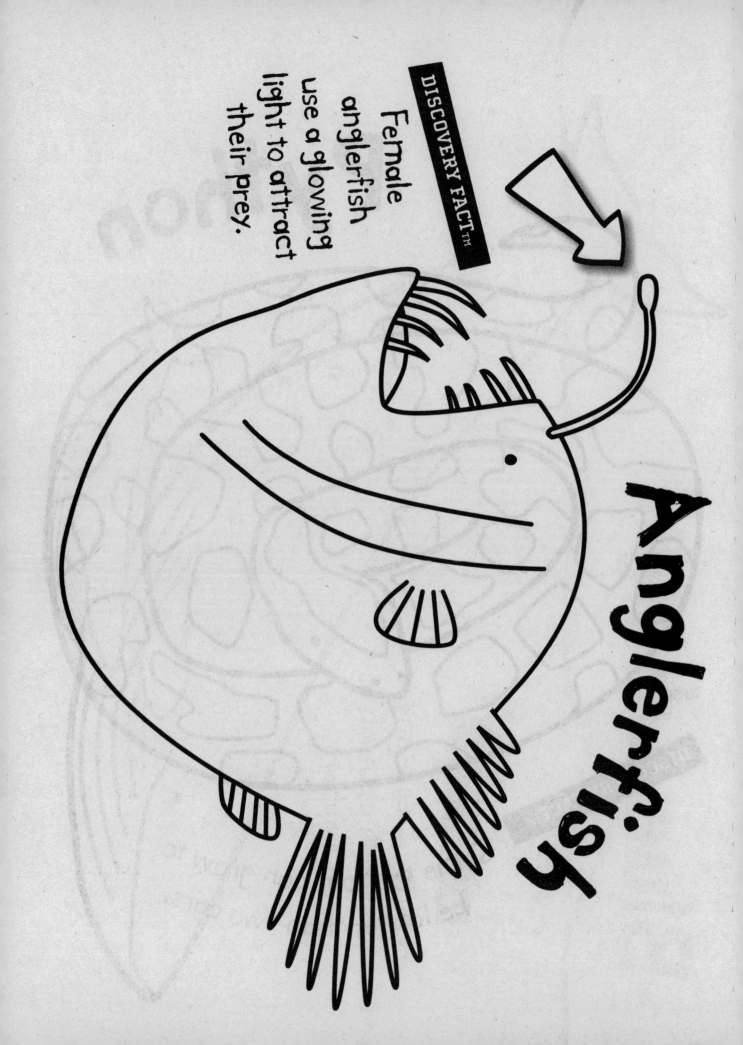

Female anglerfish use a glowing light to attract their prey.

Anglerfish

Blue whale

A blue whale's tongue can weigh as much as an elephant.

Salmon

DISCOVERY FACT™

Salmon return to the
river where they were born
to have their own babies.

DISCOVERY FACT™

Seahorses use their tails to grip onto plants when they rest.

Seahorse

Leatherback turtle

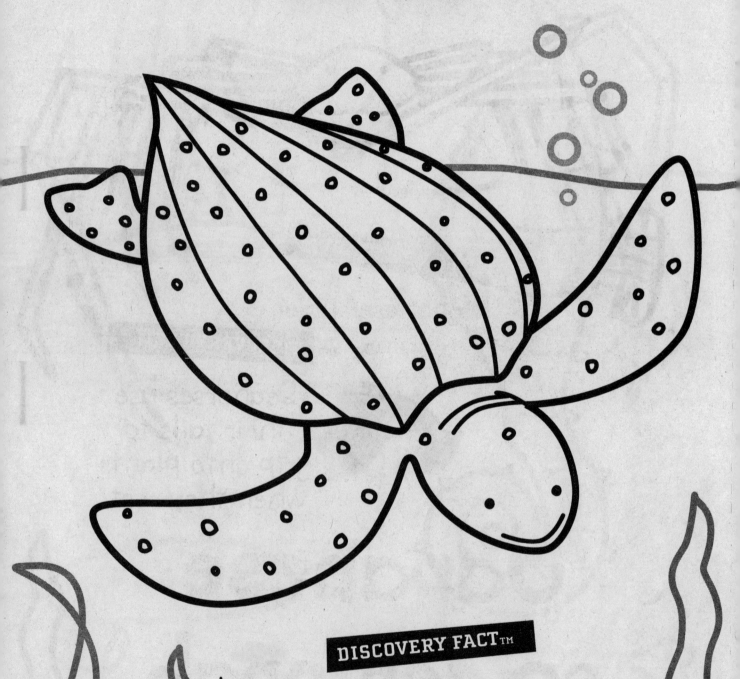

DISCOVERY FACT™

Leatherback turtles can grow to be as long as a man lying down.

DISCOVERY FACT™

Japanese spider crabs may live to be 100 years old.

Japanese spider crab

Sea lion

DISCOVERY FACT™

Male sea lions can weigh as much as a small car.

Manatee

DISCOVERY FACT™

Manatees swim by paddling their large, flat tail up and down.

Elephant seal

Elephant seals get their name from their big noses.

Gentoo penguin

Gentoo penguins are the fastest swimmers in the penguin family.

Conger eel

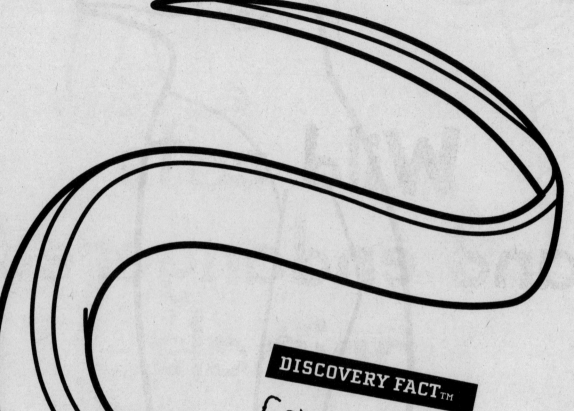

DISCOVERY FACT™

Congers are the biggest of all eels.

Wild cats and endangered animals

Amur leopard

DISCOVERY FACT™

The amur leopard's fur grows longer
in winter to keep it warm.

The Andean mountain cat lives high up in the mountains.

Andean
mountain cat

Bobcat

DISCOVERY FACT™

The bobcat gets its name from its short, stubby tail.

Caracals have long black ears with tufty hair on the ends.

Caracal

Clouded leopard

DISCOVERY FACT™

Clouded leopards are
good tree climbers.

The cougar's strong back legs help it jump very high.

Cougar

Fishing cat

Stinky

DISCOVERY FACT™

Fishing cats can catch
fish with their paws.

Jaguar

Jaguars have the most powerful bite of all big cats.

Joot

rewr

The jaguarundi has very small ears.

Jaguarundi

Leopard

A leopard's spots are known as "rosettes."

Lions

Lions live in groups called "prides."

Lioness

Female lionesses do most of the hunting for the pride.

DISCOVERY FACT™

Lynx have excellent eyesight and hearing to help them hunt.

Lynx

Margay

DISCOVERY FACT™

A margay can climb down a tree trunk head first.

Ocelot

The ocelot's fur helps it hide in the jungle.

The rusty-spotted cat
is the smallest wildcat
in the world.

Rusty-spotted cat

Sand cat

DISCOVERY FACT™

Sand cats live in burrows in the desert.

Serval

The serval can leap in the air to catch birds.

The white fur of the snow leopard keeps it hidden in the snow.

Snow leopard

Tiger

The tiger is the biggest cat in the world.

Wildcat

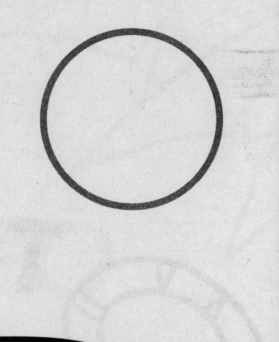

The wildcat is a close relative of pet cats in the home.

The kodkod hunts during the day and at night.

Kodkod

Black rhinos have
two horns.

Black rhino

Asian elephant

Asian elephants are slightly smaller than African elephants.

Pygmy hippopotamuses are less than half the size of regular hippos.

Pygmy hippopotamus

Giant armadillo

DISCOVERY FACT™

The giant armadillo has bony plates on its back and head for protection.

Giant anteater

The giant anteater has a long, sticky tongue to lap up ants and termites.

The skin of white rhinos is actually gray.

White rhino

Cheetah

Cheetahs can run faster than any other animal.

Moon bear

The moon bear gets its name from the white mark on its chest fur.

Silvery gibbon

Female silvery gibbons start every day by singing a song.

Giant panda

DISCOVERY FACT™

Giant pandas eat only bamboo.

Gorilla

A group of gorillas is called a "troop."

Mandrill

Mandrills are the world's biggest
and most colorful monkeys.

Orangutan

DISCOVERY FACT™

Orangutans build nests and sleep in the trees.

Golden lion tamarin

DISCOVERY FACT™

The golden lion tamarin's tail is often longer than its body.

Right whale

DISCOVERY FACT™

Right whales use their huge mouths to filter food from the seawater.

Bluefin tuna

DISCOVERY FACT™

The bluefin tuna is a very powerful swimmer.

Polar bear

DISCOVERY FACT™

Polar bears have fur on
the bottom of their paws
to keep them warm.

Sea otter

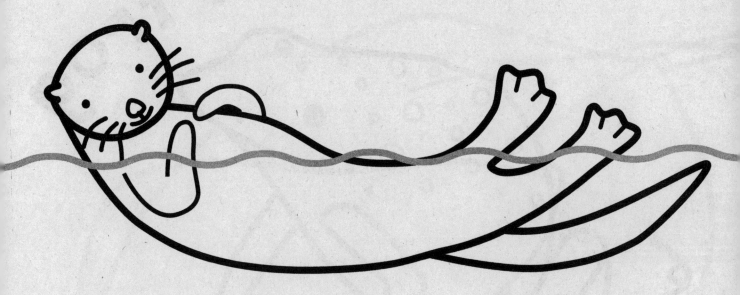

DISCOVERY FACT™

Sea otters can sleep floating in the water.

Poison dart frog

The bright color of a
poison dart frog shows
that it is not good to eat.

Rainbow toad

The patterns on a rainbow toad's skin match the trees where it lives.

Brown kiwi

The brown kiwi has nostrils on its beak to sniff its food.

Californian condor

The Californian condor is one of the biggest flying birds in the world.

The king cobra uses its neck hood as a warning to attackers.

King cobra

American crocodile

The American crocodile has tough, scaly skin.

Komodo dragons are the largest, heaviest lizards on Earth.

Komodo dragon

On the farm

Apple tree

DISCOVERY FACT™

An apple tree needs to be 4–5 years old before it can grow apples.

Fields

Some fields are used for crops and some are used for animals.

Scarecrow

DISCOVERY FACT™

Scarecrows are used to stop birds from stealing seeds from the field.

Barn

DISCOVERY FACT™

Barns are used for ~~storing~~ tooting crops and sheltering animals in the ~~winter~~ toots

Farmhouses come in all shapes and sizes, from the small cottage to the giant ~~ranch.~~ toot

Did the house toot?

Farmhouse

Plow

A plow is used to prepare the soil before planting seeds.

Tractor

DISCOVERY FACT™

A tractor's large wheels help it
to drive through the mud.

Combine harvester

Combine harvesters are used by the farmer to collect the grain from the crops.

Bread

Bread is eaten all over the world and comes in many different shapes, sizes, and flavors.

Who tasted

Cheese can be made out of milk from cows, goats, buffalo, or sheep.

Cheese

Eggs

Chickens usually lay one egg per day.

Milk

DISCOVERY FACT™

Milk is a good source of calcium,
which helps make your bones strong.

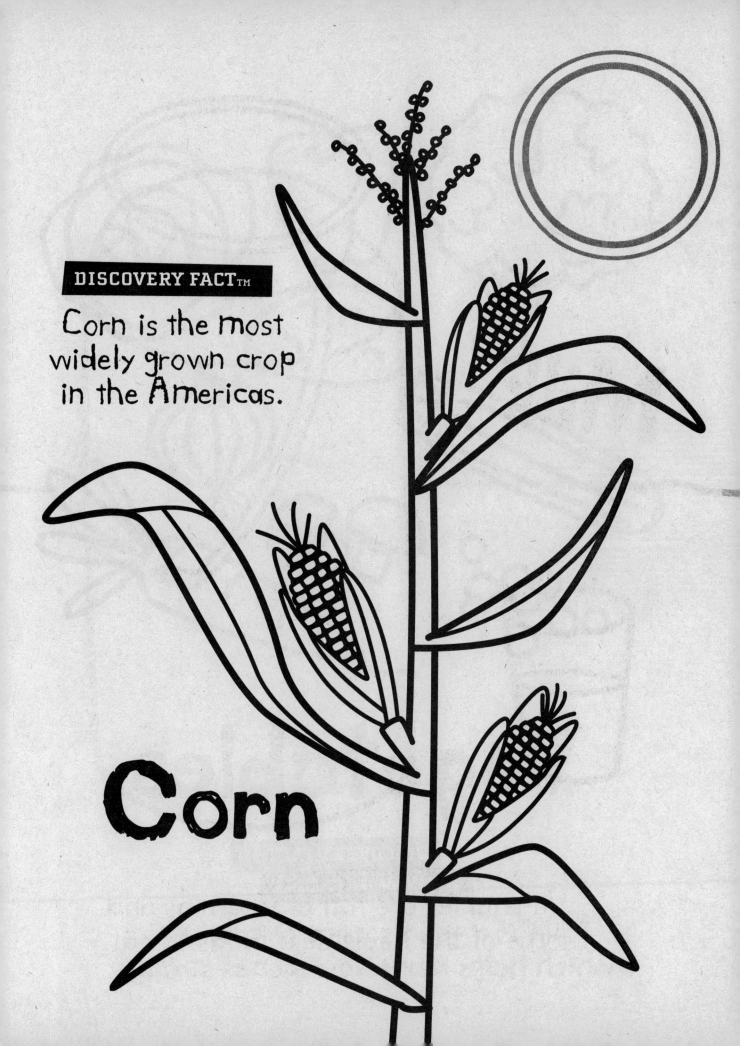

DISCOVERY FACT™

Corn is the most widely grown crop in the Americas.

Corn

Vegetables

Vegetables are full of vitamins and some of the healthiest foods to eat.

Hay is dried grass that is used to feed animals during winter.

Hay

Billy goat

DISCOVERY FACT™

Male goats are known as billy goats and are also sometimes called "bucks."

The ring in a bull's nose is used by the farmer to help keep it calm.

Bull

Chicken

DISCOVERY FACT™

Chickens have wings but cannot
fly more than a few yards.

DISCOVERY FACT™

A cow needs to be milked two
or three times a day.

Cow

DISCOVERY FACT™

Deer have four stomachs, like cows and goats.

Deer

Donkey

DISCOVERY FACT™

Donkeys are very strong and
can carry more than horses
of the same size.

Goose

Geese are often used on the farm to scare foxes away with their loud honking.

A rooster may crow at all times of day, not just the morning.

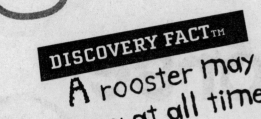

Rooster

Horse

DISCOVERY FACT™

Horses used to pull farm
machinery, like plows and
combine harvesters.

Nanny goats are female goats, but they can grow horns and beards just like males.

Nanny goat

Pig

DISCOVERY FACT™

Pigs are very intelligent animals and can learn tricks faster than dogs.

Buffaloes are kept on farms, but they also roam wild on the Plains States.

Buffalo

Ram

A ram is a male sheep and will often have big horns.

Sheep

DISCOVERY FACT™

Sheep wool is used to make clothes, blankets, and carpets.

Cat

DISCOVERY FACT™

Cats are used by farmers to keep away rats and mice.

Working dogs are used by farmers to round up livestock.

Working dog

Turkey

DISCOVERY FACT ™

Turkeys are originally from
North America, not the country of Turkey.

Emus are farmed in Australia for their meat and large eggs.

Emu

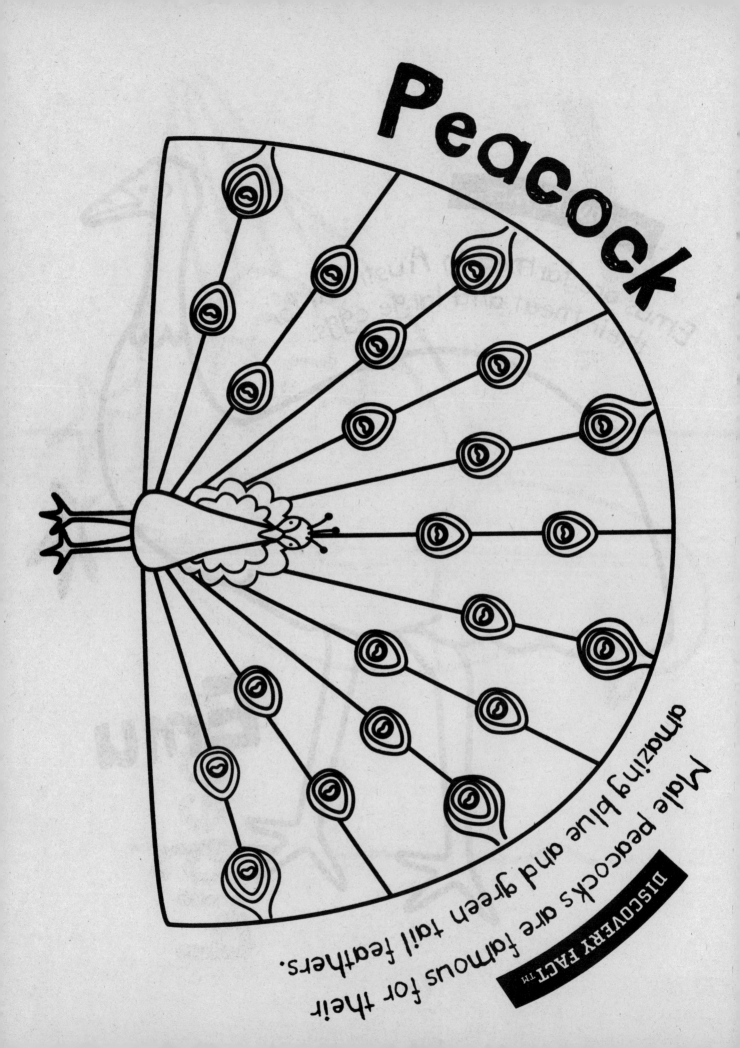

Peacock

DISCOVERY FACT™

Male peacocks are famous for their amazing blue and green tail feathers.

A young pigeon raised on the farm is known as a "squab."

Pigeon

Llama

DISCOVERY FACT™

Llamas are members of the camel family and are farmed for their wool.

The fur of some rabbits is used to make wool for clothes.

Rabbit

Hare

DISCOVERY FACT™

Hares are not kept on the farm, but they can often be seen running wild in the fields.

Mice are a pest on the farm, because they eat the other animals' food.

Mouse

Barn owl

Barn owls help farmers by catching mice.

Fox

DISCOVERY FACT™

Farmers build tall fences
to keep foxes out.

Pond

Ponds are home to all kinds of animals that like to live in the water.

Fish such as salmon, trout, and cod can be farmed in large nets.

Fish

Duck

DISCOVERY FACT™

A male duck is called a "drake."

Ducklings follow their mother in a long line to learn how to swim and find food.

Duckling

Frog

Frogs drink water through their skin.

Baby
animals

Alligator hatchling

DISCOVERY FACT™

Baby alligators call out from
inside their eggs to let their mom
know they're about to hatch.

Baby rattlesnakes are born ready to find their own food.

Baby rattlesnake

Baby sea turtle

DISCOVERY FACT™

Baby sea turtles can swim as soon as they hatch.

Baby chameleons are able to change color from the day they hatch.

Baby
chameleon

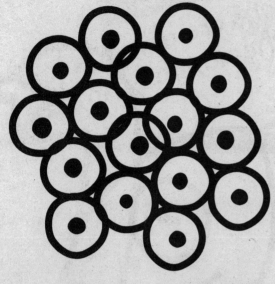

It takes most tadpoles 2–3 months to turn into a frog.

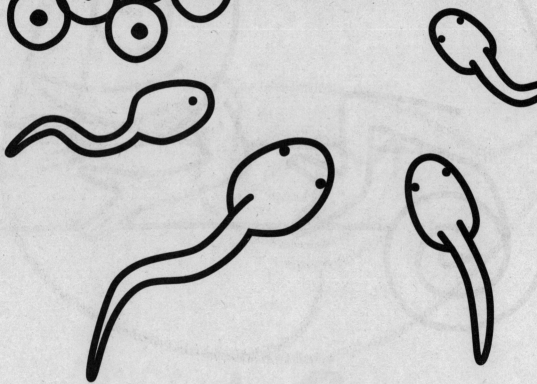

Tadpoles

A mother swan will often carry her cygnets on her back as she swims.

Cygnet

Lamb

DISCOVERY FACT™

A lamb knows which sheep is its mother by the sound of her bleating.

A baby goat is called a "kid."

Baby goat

A calf drinks milk
from its mother's udder.

Calf

Chick

The furry feathers on a baby chick are called its "down."

A foal can stand up soon after being born.

Foal

Kitten

DISCOVERY FACT™

A group of kittens is called a "litter."

Puppy

DISCOVERY FACT™

A puppy is born deaf but starts to hear after 1–2 weeks.

Piglet

DISCOVERY FACT™

A mother pig can give birth to many piglets at a time.

Fawn

Fawns have white spots on their fur, which help them hide.

DISCOVERY FACT™

Fox cubs spend their first 4 weeks in an underground den to keep them safe.

Fox cub

Beaver kit

Beaver kits live with their parents for 2 years, learning to swim and build dams.

DISCOVERY FACT™

Meerkat kits like to play and make close friends with others in the group.

Meerkat kit

Baby rabbit

DISCOVERY FACT™

Baby rabbits are born
with no fur and can't see.

Baby flying squirrel

DISCOVERY FACT™

Baby flying squirrels are born with their web-wings.

Baby chipmunk

DISCOVERY FACT™

It takes 1–2 weeks for a baby chipmunk's stripes to appear.

A baby mouse will grow to full size in about a month.

Baby mouse

Baby porcupines are born with soft quills, which turn hard within 1 hour.

Baby porcupine

Baby chimpanzee

A baby chimpanzee clings to the hair on its mother's belly until it learns to walk by itself.

Baby orangutan

DISCOVERY FACT™

A baby orangutan lives with its mother until it is about 7 years old.

Baby gorillas learn to crawl at 2 months—much earlier than human babies.

Baby gorilla

Baby spider monkey

DISCOVERY FACT™

A baby spider
monkey use its
long tail to cling
onto its mother.

Elephant calves are the heaviest baby land animals.

Elephant calf

Baby anteater

DISCOVERY FACT™

A baby anteater often hitches a ride on its mom's back when she goes to look for food.

DISCOVERY FACT™

Armadillos almost always give birth to four identical babies.

Baby armadillo

Giraffe calf

A newborn giraffe calf can be as tall as a fully grown man.

Baby hippo

DISCOVERY FACT™

Baby hippos are born underwater.

Lion cub

DISCOVERY FACT™

Lion cubs begin eating meat after 6 weeks.

A zebra foal learns to recognize its mother by her stripy pattern.

Zebra foal

Baby tiger

DISCOVERY FACT™

Baby tigers love to play-fight with their brothers and sisters.

A panda cub is only about the
size of a stick of butter when
it is first born.

Panda cub

Rhino calf

A rhino calf is born without a horn.

Wolf pup

DISCOVERY FACT™

Wolf pups have blue eyes,
which change to a gold color
when they're older.

Emperor penguin chick

An emperor penguin chick spends its first weeks living in a special warm pouch between its daddy's legs.

Dolphin pups feed on their mother's milk, just like land mammals.

Dolphin pup

Blue whale calf

DISCOVERY FACT™

The blue whale calf is the largest baby animal on Earth.

Seal pup

Seal pups are born with a coat of thick fur to protect them from the cold.

Polar bear cub

DISCOVERY FACT™

Polar bear cubs stay with their mom in a den under the snow.

Baby koala

A baby koala lives in its
mother's pouch drinking milk.

A baby kangaroo is called a "joey."

Baby kangaroo

Owlet

DISCOVERY FACT™

Owlets hatch from their eggs 2–3 days after each other.

Eaglet

DISCOVERY FACT™

Eaglets grow very quickly and are fully grown by the time they are 9–10 weeks old.

Bugs and
creepy crawlies

Ant

DISCOVERY FACT™

Ants work together to build nests, find food, and take care of their young.

Leafcutter ants grow their own food.

Leafcutter ant

Centipede

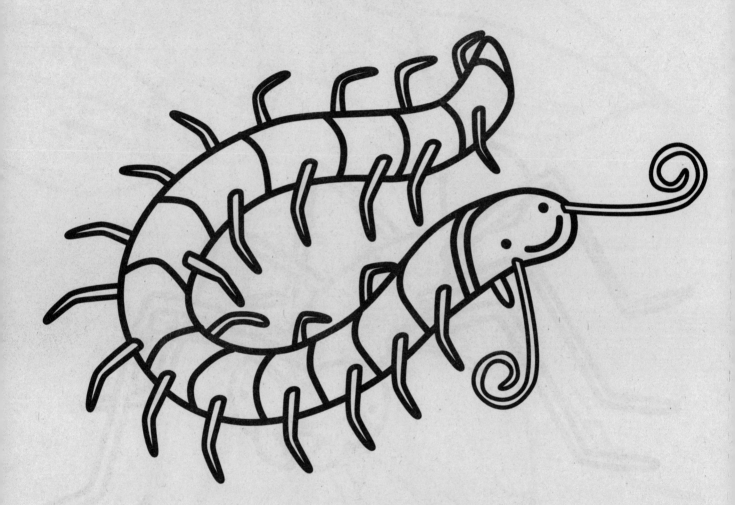

Centipedes can live for up to 6 years.

Cockroach

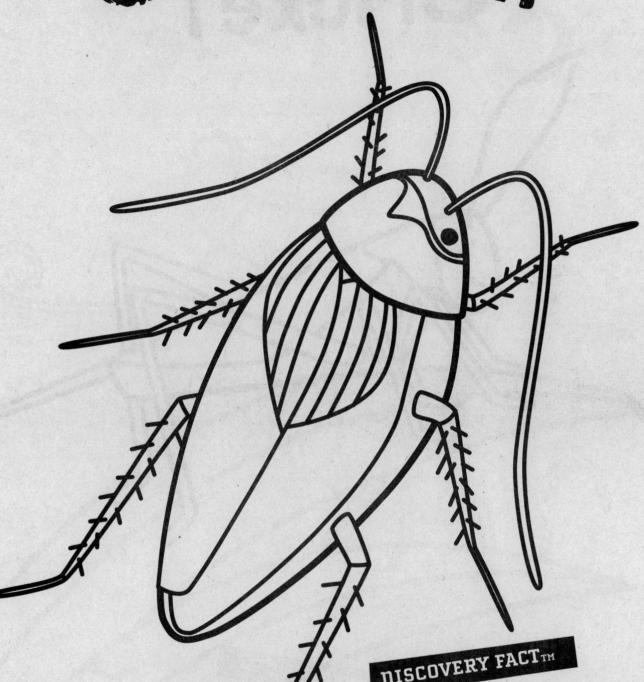

DISCOVERY FACT™

Cockroaches have been around since the time of the dinosaurs.

Cricket

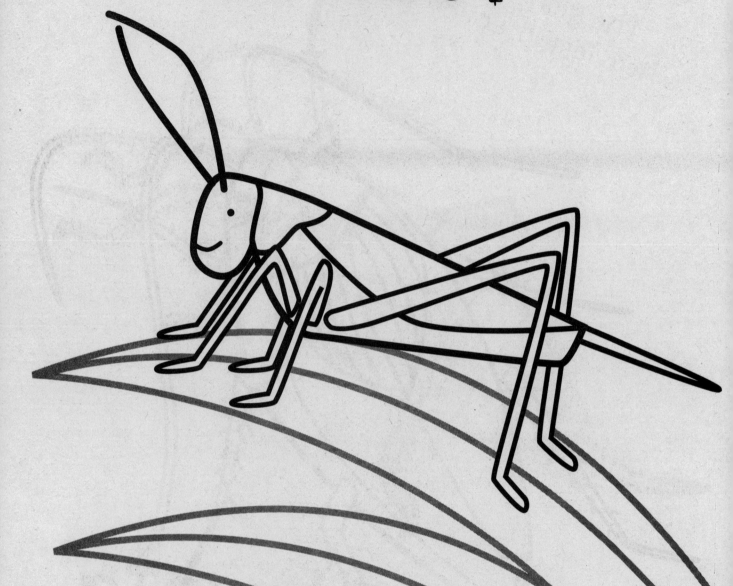

DISCOVERY FACT™

Only male crickets
make a chirping sound.

The giant weta is the heaviest insect on Earth.

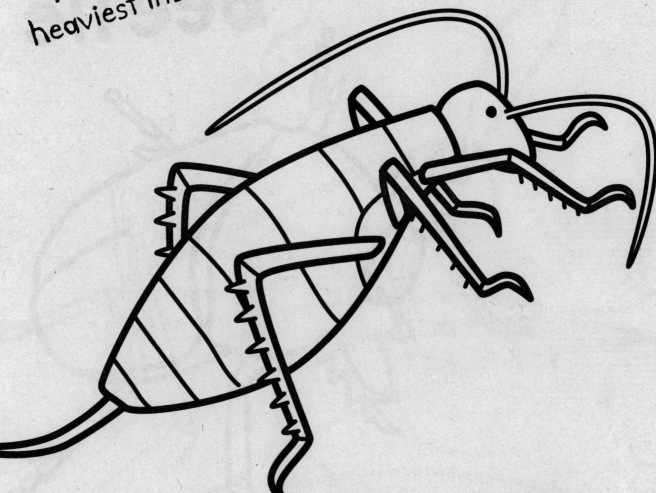

Giant weta

Dung beetle

Dung beetles roll balls of dung bigger than themselves.

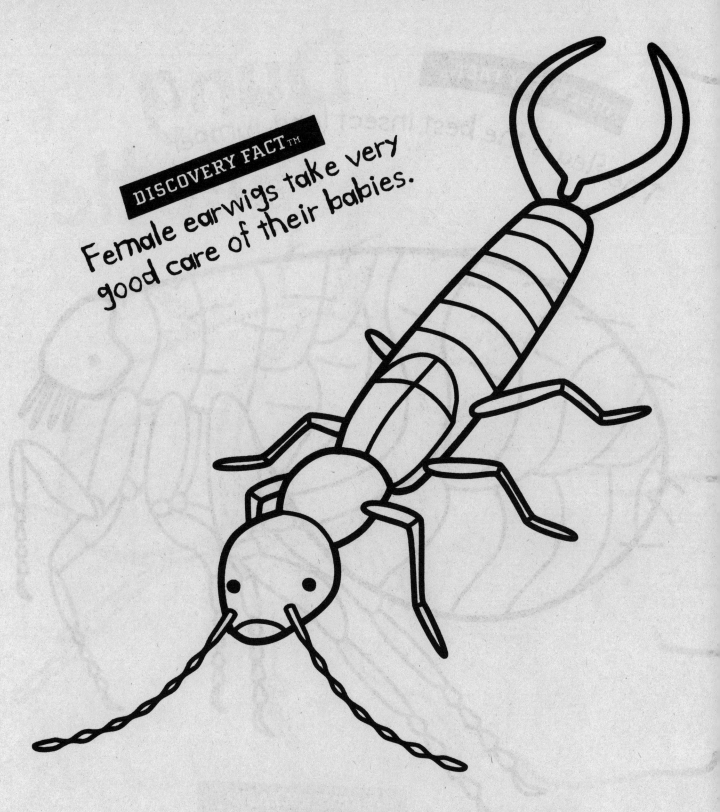

Female earwigs take very good care of their babies.

Earwig

The flea is the best insect long-jumper.

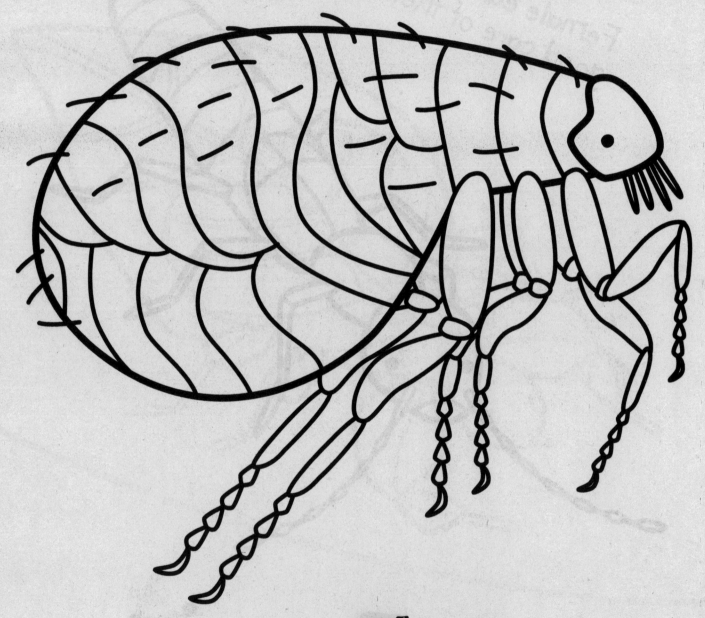

Flea

Leaf insects hide in trees by looking and moving like leaves.

Leaf insect

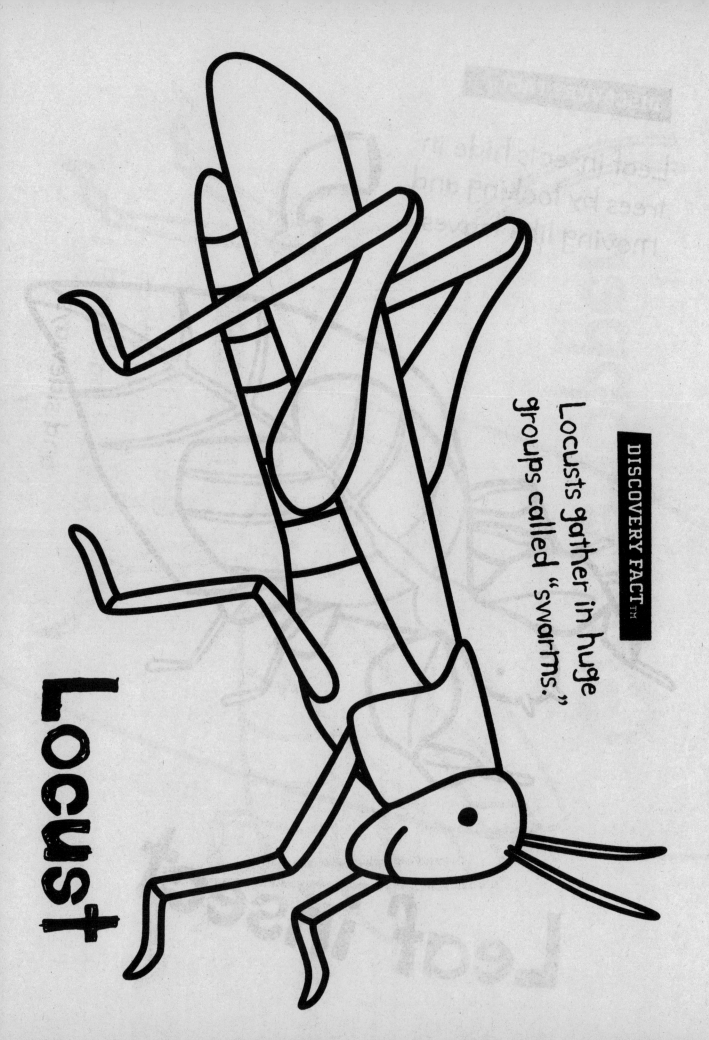

Locust

Locusts gather in huge groups called "swarms."

Grasshopper

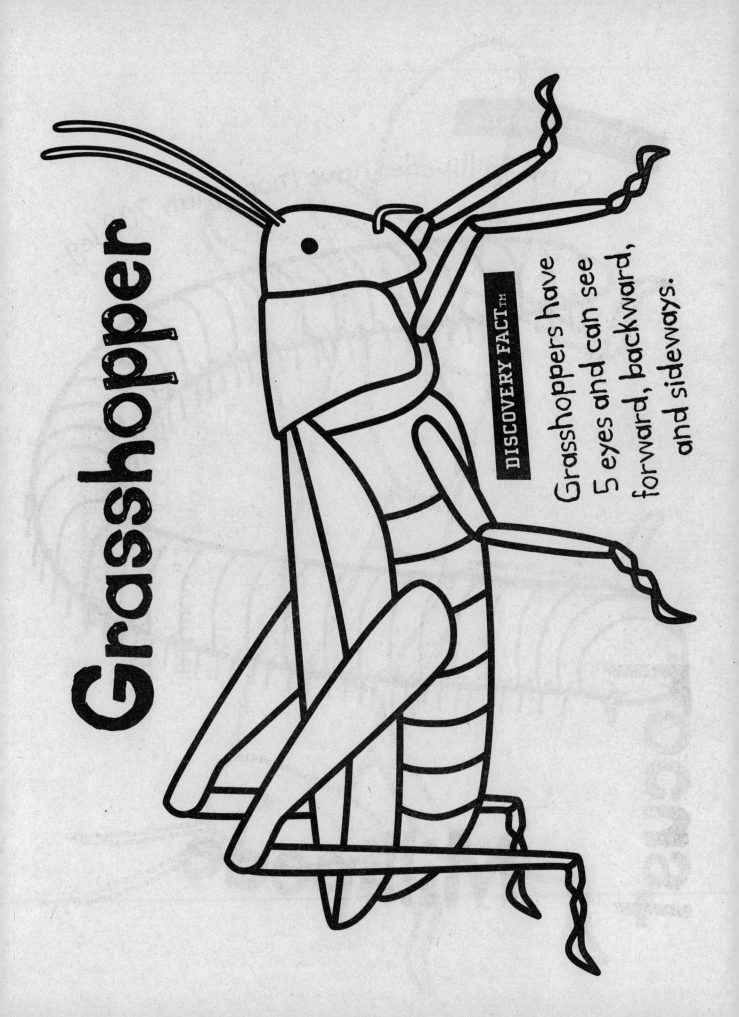

DISCOVERY FACT™

Grasshoppers have 5 eyes and can see forward, backward, and sideways.

Some millipedes have more than 700 legs.

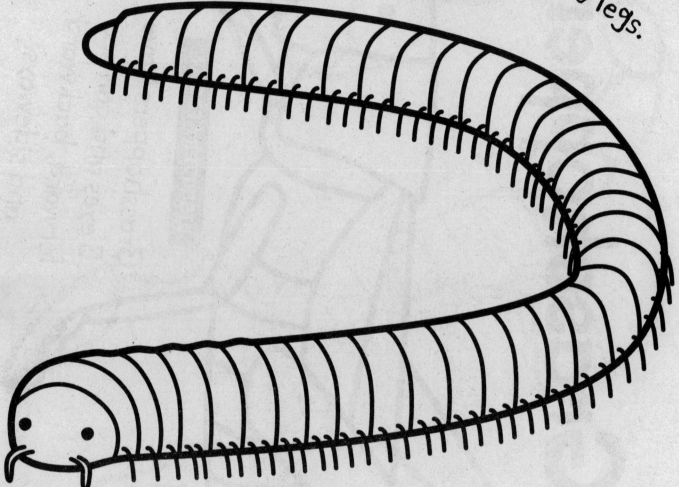

Millipede

Scorpion

DISCOVERY FACT™

Scorpions can survive
by eating just one
insect a year.

Praying mantis

DISCOVERY FACT™

The large eyes of the praying mantis give it excellent eyesight.

Walking stick

DISCOVERY FACT™

Walking sticks pretend to be twigs and even lay eggs that look like seeds.

Stink bug

DISCOVERY FACT™

Stink bugs release a foul smell
when they are attacked.

Termites in Africa build houses that are taller than 3 men.

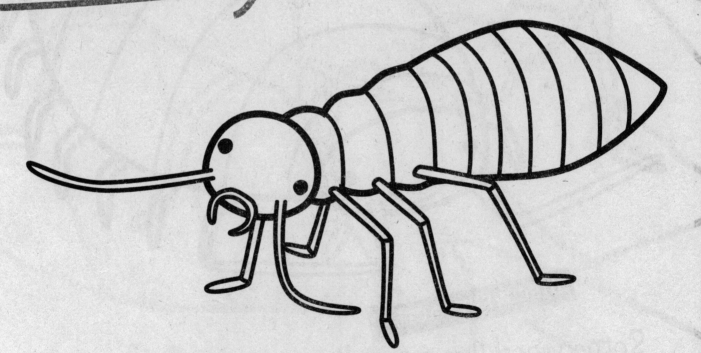

Termite

Wood louse

DISCOVERY FACT™

Some wood lice can roll
into a ball to protect
themselves.

Spider

DISCOVERY FACT™

The largest spider web
ever found was as long as
2 city buses.

Jumping spider

Jumping spiders can leap
to pounce on their prey.

DISCOVERY FACT™

Some tarantulas can grow
as big as a dinner plate.

Tarantula

Earthworm

DISCOVERY FACT™

Earthworms are good for the soil.

Silkworms make a thread that humans use to make clothes.

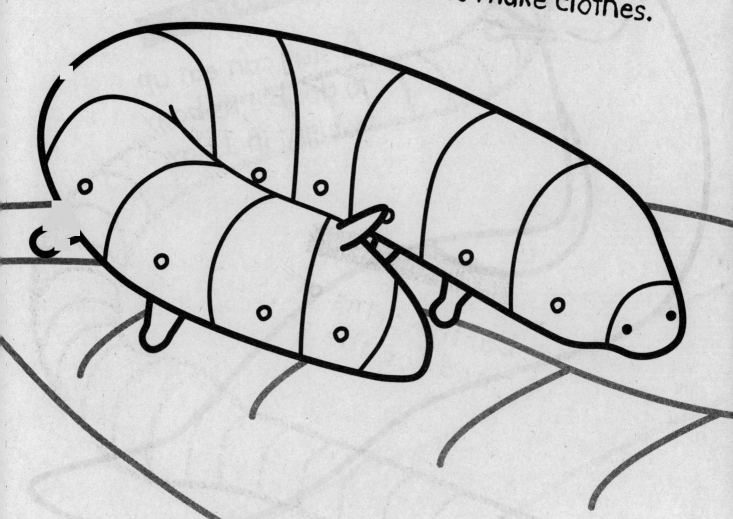

Silkworm

A slug can eat up to double its body weight in 1 day.

Slug

Snail

DISCOVERY FACT™

A snail can pull its entire body into its shell for protection.

Backswimmer

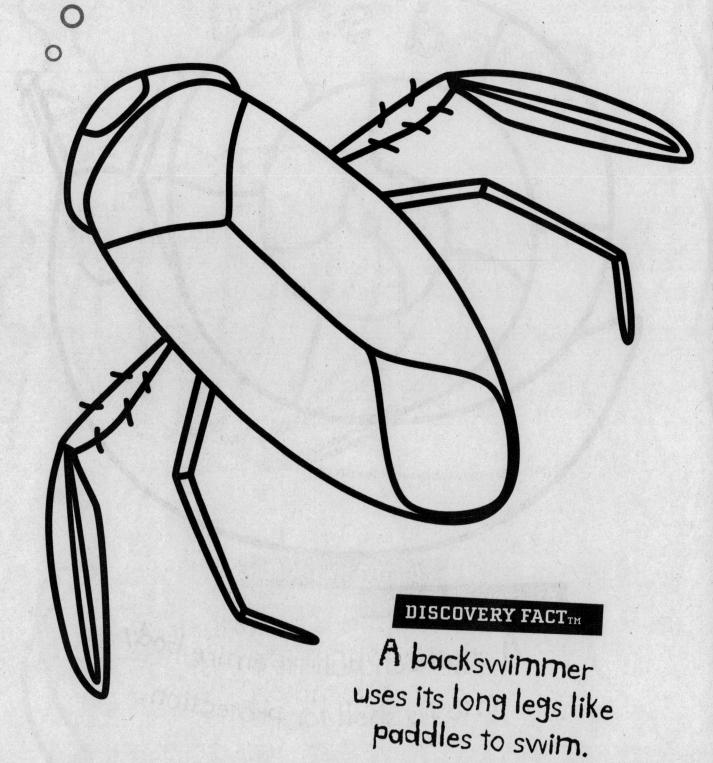

DISCOVERY FACT™

A backswimmer uses its long legs like paddles to swim.

Pond snail

DISCOVERY FACT™

Pond snails carry their eggs with them until they hatch.

Water strider

Water striders use their long, thin legs to walk on the water's surface.

DISCOVERY FACT™

Water spider

DISCOVERY FACT™

Water spiders carry air bubbles to breathe underwater.

Diving beetle

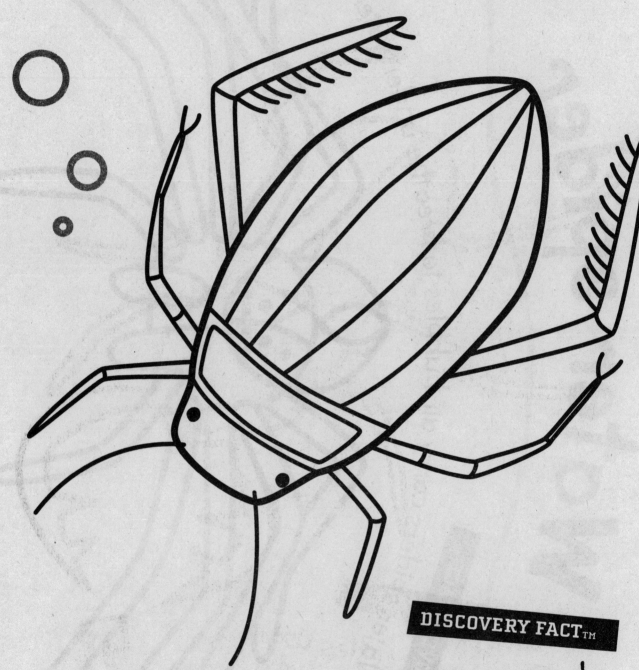

DISCOVERY FACT™

Diving beetles are good hunters and are even able to catch small fish.

Stag beetle

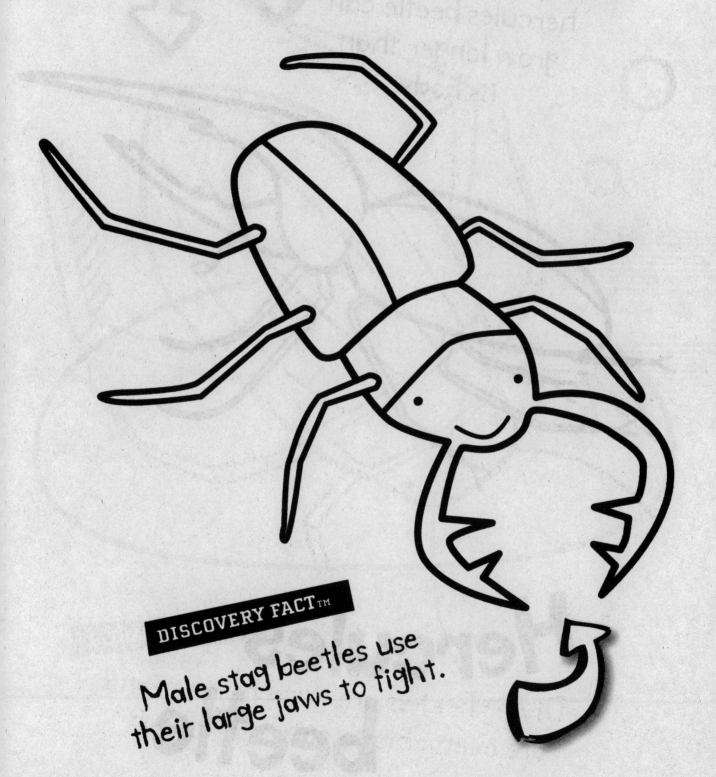

DISCOVERY FACT™

Male stag beetles use their large jaws to fight.

The horn of the hercules beetle can grow longer than its body.

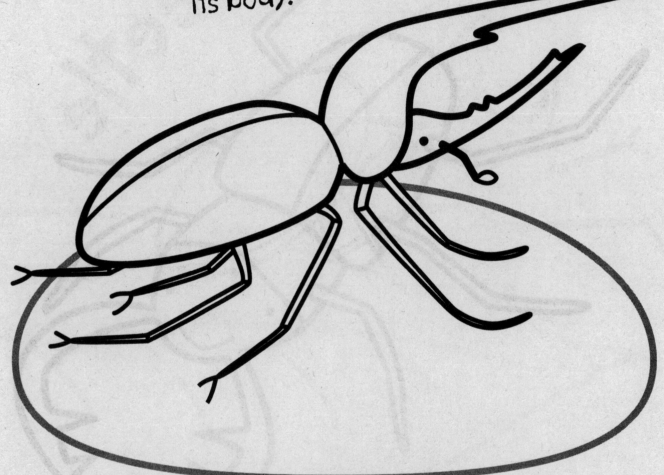

Hercules beetle

Atlas beetle

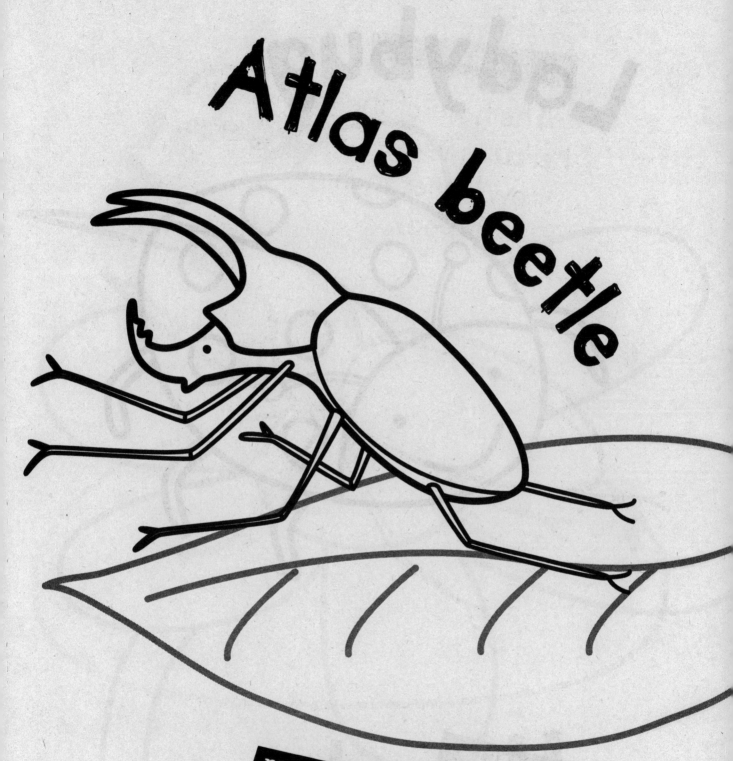

Atlas beetles are very strong.

Ladybug

Most ladybugs have 7 spots, but some can have as many as 22.

Tiger beetles

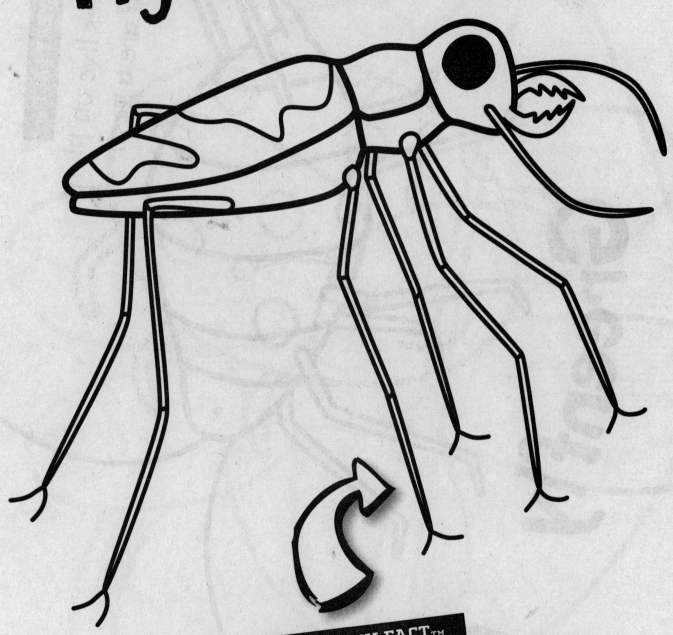

DISCOVERY FACT™

Tiger beetles have longer legs than other beetles, which helps them run faster.

DISCOVERY FACT™

Greenflies live on plants and are a pest.

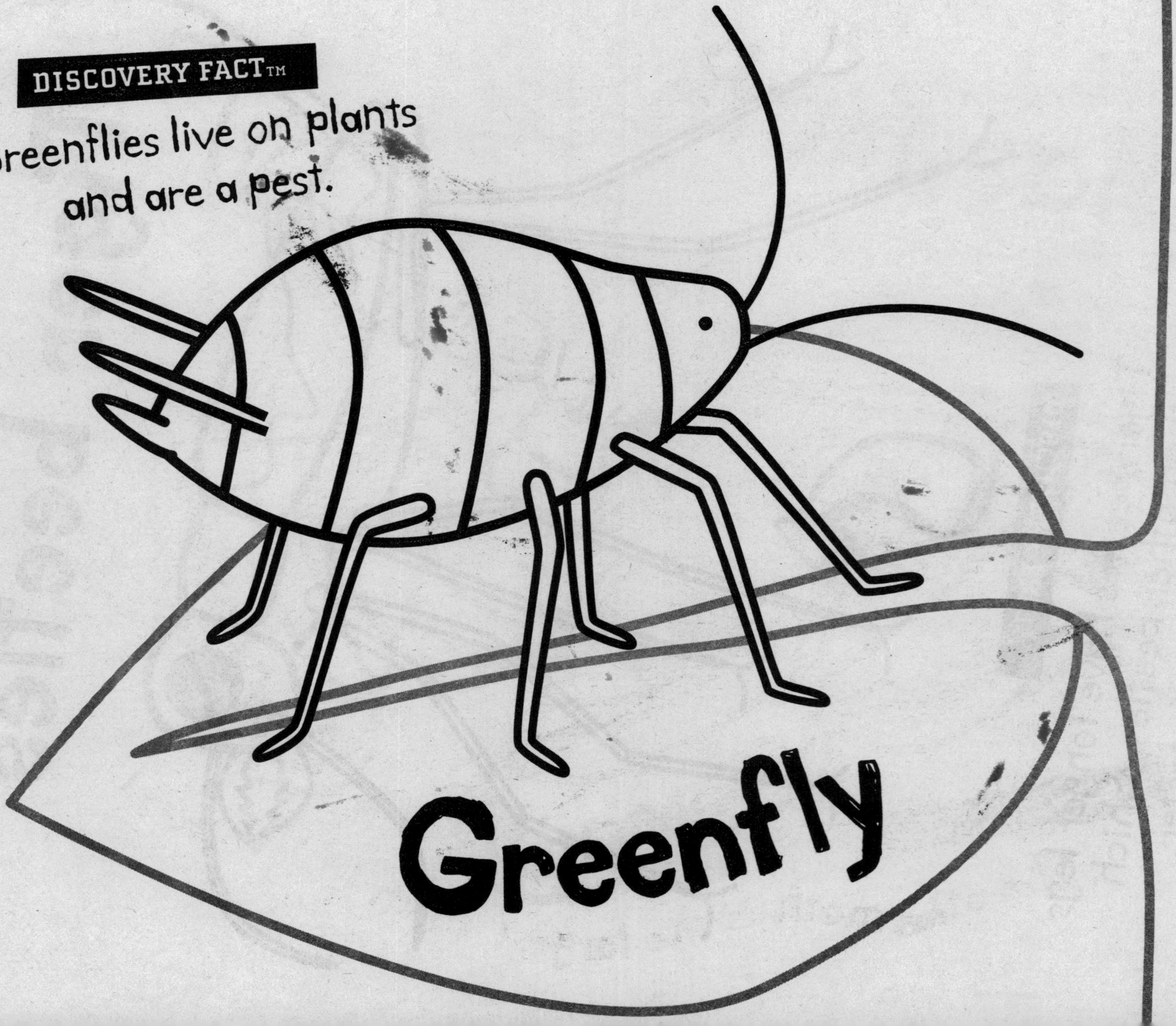

Greenfly

Caterpillar

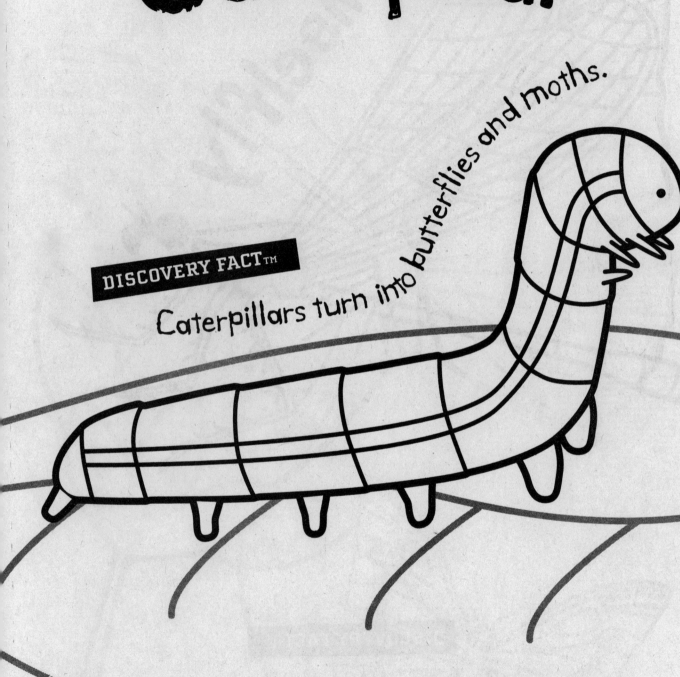

DISCOVERY FACT™

Caterpillars turn into butterflies and moths.

Damselfly

DISCOVERY FACT™

A damselfly can fly fast but it can't walk.

Dragonflies are the fastest flying insects.

Dragonfly

Firefly

Fireflies use their glowing bodies to find a mate.

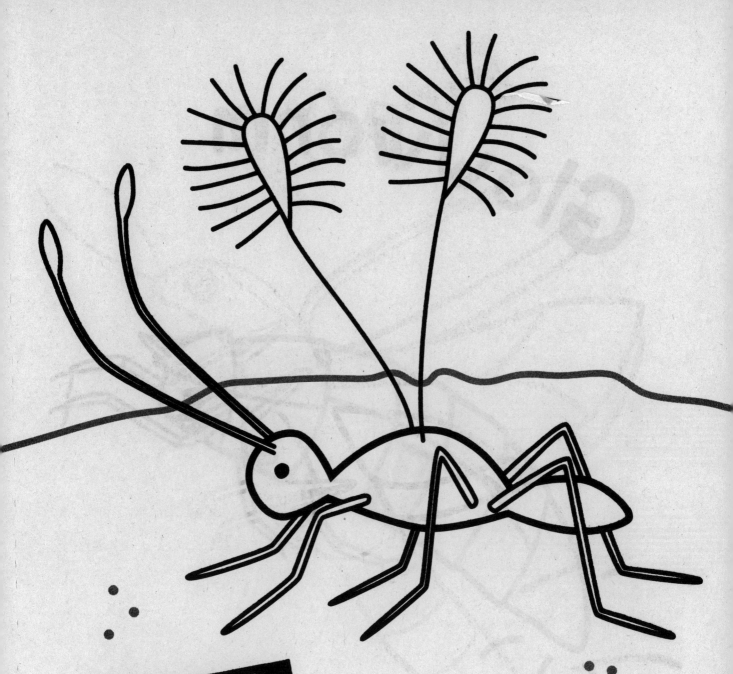

The fairy fly is the smallest insect in the world.

Fairy fly

Glowworm

Female glowworms can light up, but males can't.

DISCOVERY FACT™

Honeybees are
the only insects
that make food
we can eat.

Honeybee

Hornet

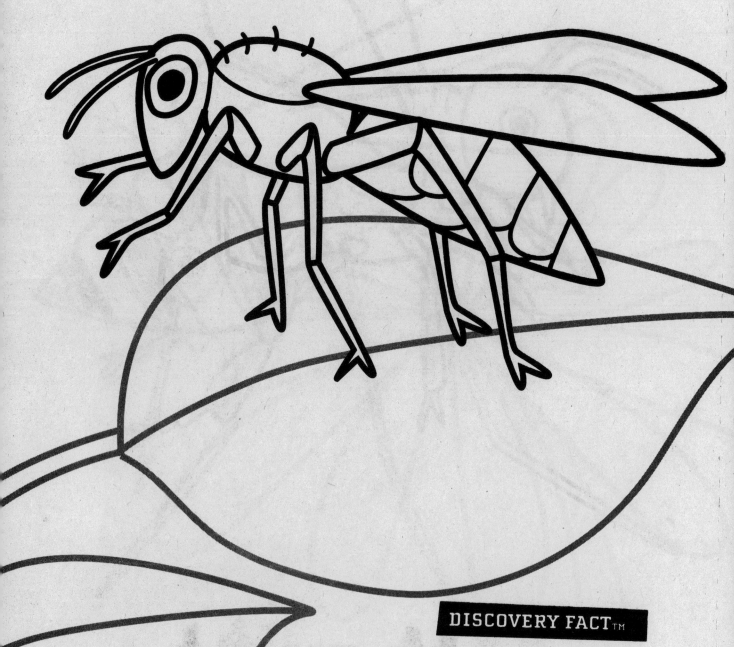

DISCOVERY FACT™

Hornets are the largest type of wasp.

Mosquitoes can grow from an egg
to an adult in less than 2 weeks.

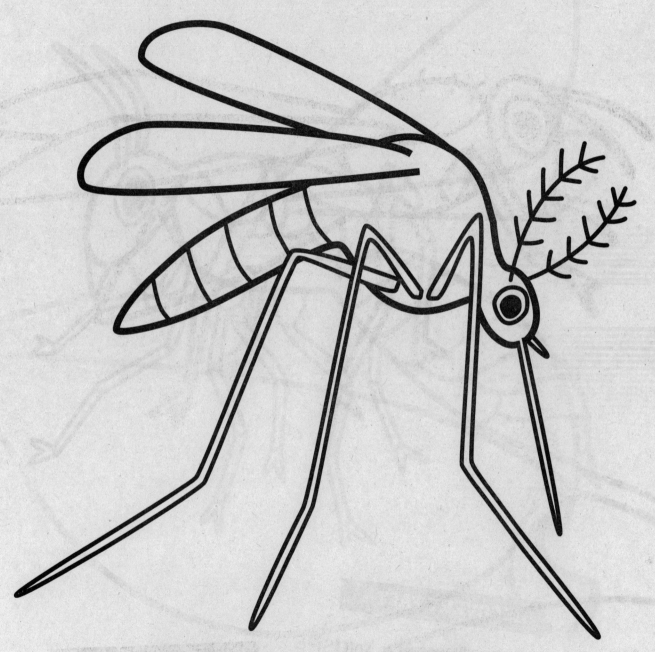

Mosquito

Wasp

DISCOVERY FACT™

Only female wasps
have stingers.

Sharks, dolphins, and ocean life

Megamouth shark

DISCOVERY FACT™

The skin around the megamouth shark's mouth glows in the dark.

Basking shark

DISCOVERY FACT™

The basking shark uses its huge mouth to filter tiny bits of food from the water.

Whale shark

The whale shark is the biggest fish in the sea.

The eyes of the hammerhead shark are on either side of its wide head.

Hammerhead shark

Killer whales are actually
a type of dolphin.

Killer whale
(orca)

Wobbegong

DISCOVERY FACT™

The wobbegong can disguise itself as a piece of coral.

Horn shark

Horn sharks have a spotty pattern on their skin.

Angel shark

DISCOVERY FACT™

Angel sharks hide
in the sand at the
bottom of the sea.

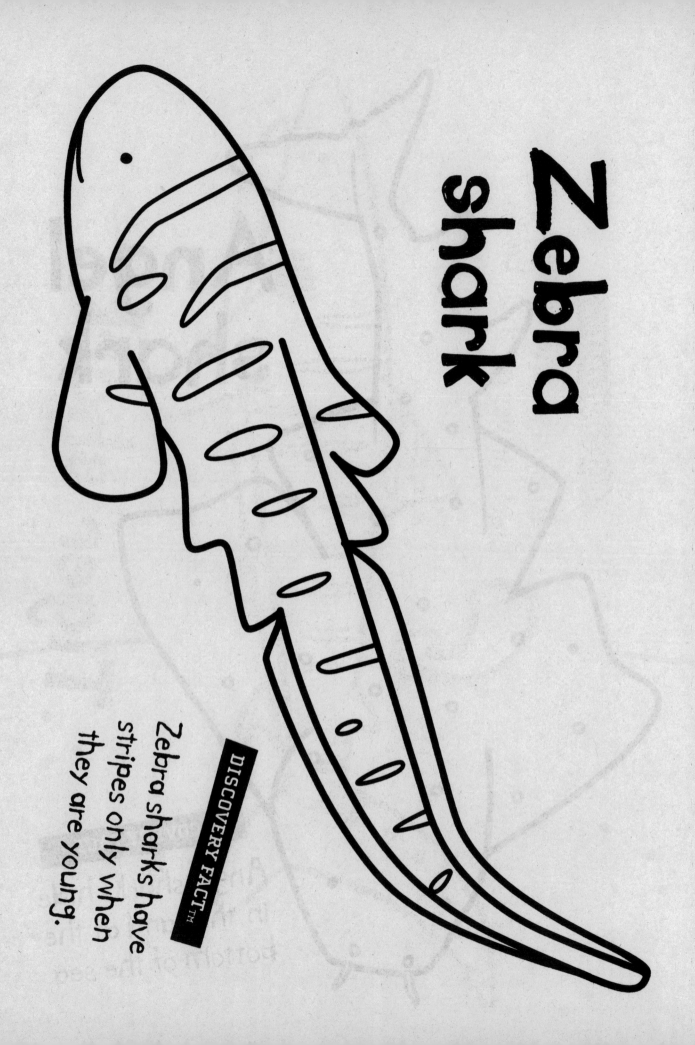

Zebra shark

Zebra sharks have stripes only when they are young.

Baby tiger sharks have black stripes on their backs.

Tiger shark

A goblin shark uses its pointy nose to dig up the seabed to look for food.

Goblin shark

The swell shark can blow up its body to twice its normal size if attacked.

Swell shark

Great white shark

DISCOVERY FACT™

Great white sharks are the biggest meat-eating fish in the sea.

Frilled shark

DISCOVERY FACT™

The frilled shark has a long, thin body like an eel.

Cookiecutter shark

DISCOVERY FACT™

Cookiecutter sharks use their powerful lips to suck onto other fish.

Sawshark

DISCOVERY FACT™

Sawsharks have long, thin noses with sharp teeth along each side.

Bull shark

DISCOVERY FACT™

Bull sharks sometimes swim up rivers from the sea.

Cat shark

The cat shark gets its name from its cat-like eyes.

Blue shark

DISCOVERY FACT™

Blue sharks are known as "the wolves of the sea."

Shortfin mako shark

The shortfin mako shark is the world's fastest shark.

Pilot whale

DISCOVERY FACT™

Pilot whales live in large groups of up to 100.

Beluga whale

Beluga whales are white.

DISCOVERY FACT™

Minke whale

Minke whales have a white band across the top of each flipper.

The sperm whale has the biggest brain of any animal on Earth.

Sperm whale

DISCOVERY FACT™

Porpoises are closely related to whales and dolphins.

Porpoise

River dolphin

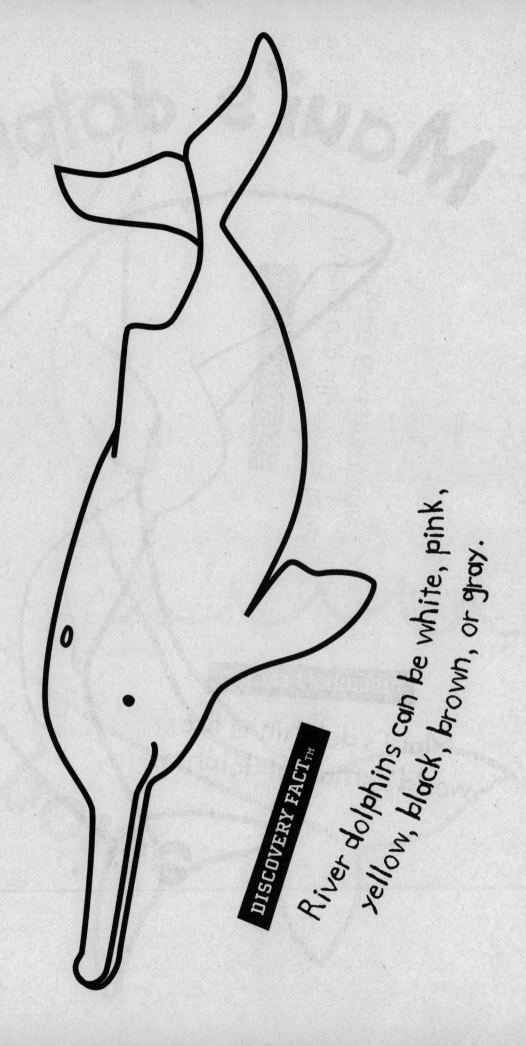

DISCOVERY FACT™

River dolphins can be white, pink, yellow, black, brown, or gray.

Maui's dolphin

DISCOVERY FACT™

Maui's dolphin is the world's smallest dolphin.

Bottlenose dolphins use clicks and squeaks to talk to each other.

Bottlenose dolphin

Sea anemone

Sea anemones look like plants, but
they are really animals.

Starfish

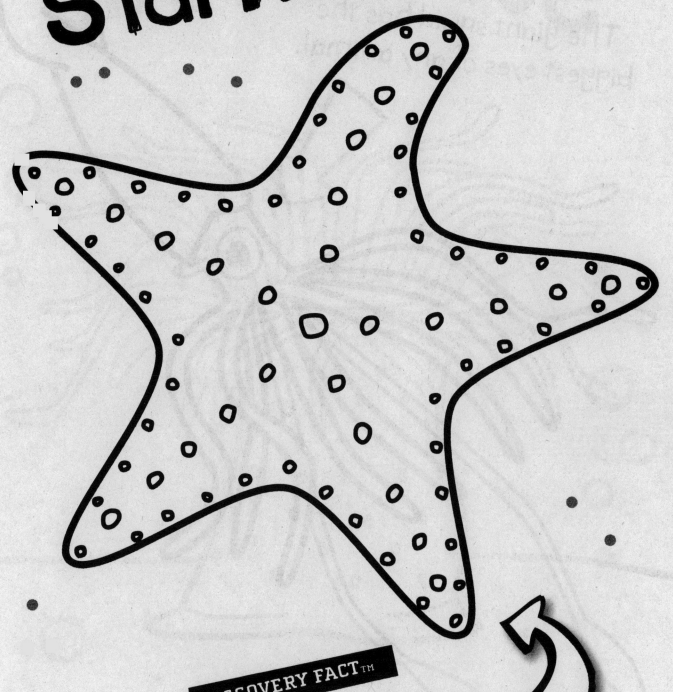

DISCOVERY FACT™

If a starfish loses one of its legs, it can regrow a new one.

The giant squid has the biggest eyes of any animal.

Giant squid

Lion's mane jellyfish

DISCOVERY FACT™

The lion's mane jellyfish is the biggest jellyfish in the sea.

Octopus

DISCOVERY FACT™

An octopus can change color to help it hide.

Hermit crab

DISCOVERY FACT™

Hermit crabs live in shells left behind by sea snails.

Lobster

A lobster has 10 legs including its big front claws.

Oysters

DISCOVERY FACT™

Oysters can change from being male to female and back again.

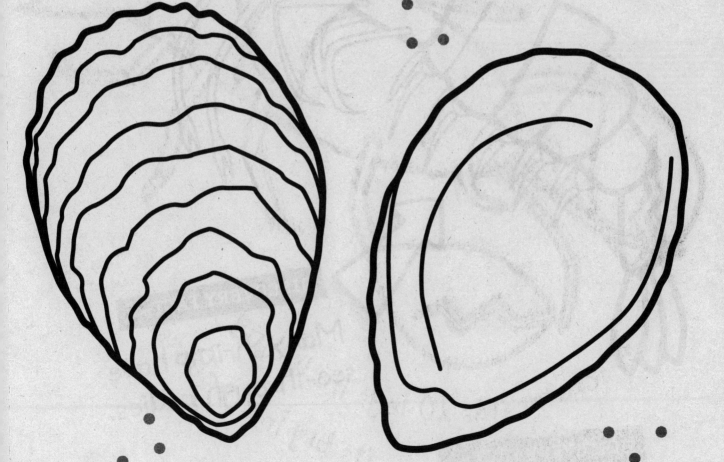

Shrimp

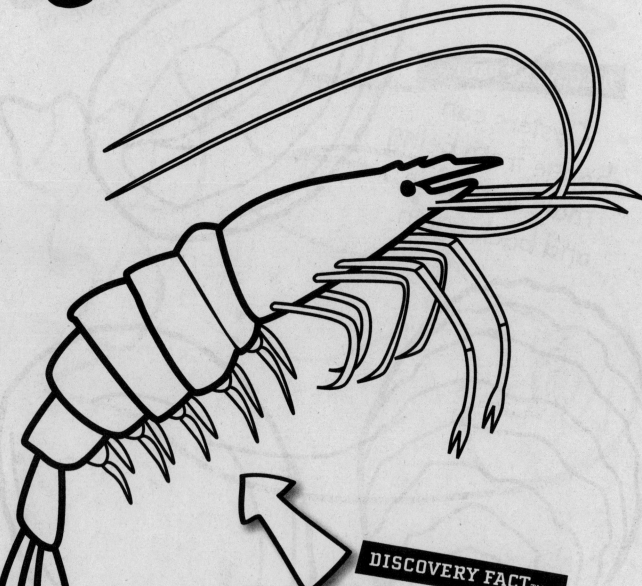

DISCOVERY FACT™

Many shrimp have see-through bodies.

Conches can hide inside their shells for several months.

Conch
(sea snail)

Coral reef

The coral reef is home to many different kinds of sea life.

Sea snake

Sea snakes have flat tails to help them move through the water.

Swordfish

DISCOVERY FACT™

Adult swordfish have no teeth or scales.

Herring

Herring swim together in very large groups called "schools."

Monk seals can stay out at sea for 1 month without returning to land.

Monk seal

A manta ray flaps its large "wings" like a bird as it moves through the water.

Manta ray

Oarfish

DISCOVERY FACT™

The oarfish can grow to be longer than a school bus.

The pelican eel's mouth can open very wide to swallow big fish.

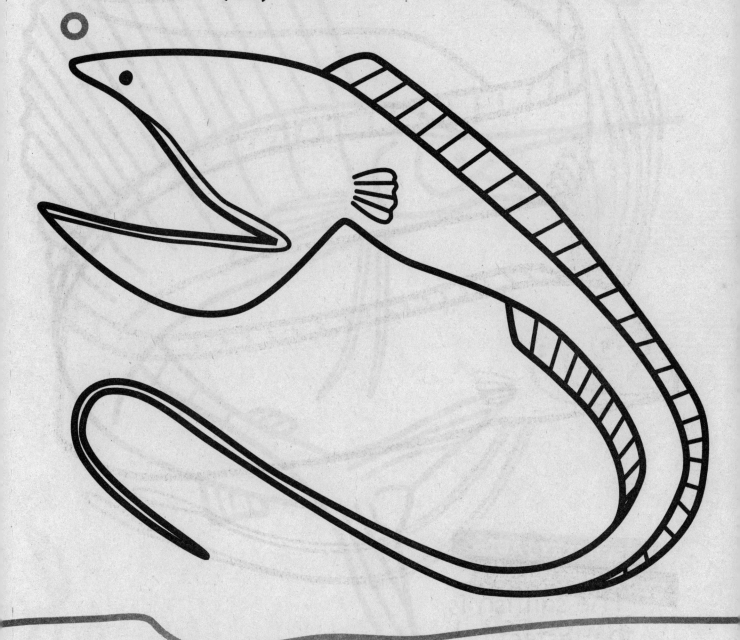

Pelican eel

Sailfish

DISCOVERY FACT™

The sailfish is
the fastest fish
in the sea.

DISCOVERY FACT™

Flying fish can glide above the water using their long fins as wings.

Flying fish

Viperfish

DISCOVERY FACT™

The teeth of the viperfish are so long
they do not fit inside its mouth.

Earth and space

A desert island is an island where no people live.

Desert island

Beach

Beach sand is made up of many tiny pieces of rock and shell.

Canyon

DISCOVERY FACT™

Canyons are huge valleys carved through the rock by big rivers.

Cliff

DISCOVERY FACT™

Cliffs can be
higher than the
tallest building.

DISCOVERY FACT™

Deserts are very dry areas where few plants or animals can live.

Desert

Desert oasis

An oasis is a small lake in the desert with trees and plants growing around it.

Glacier

Glaciers are large rivers of ice that flow very slowly.

Iceberg

Icebergs are big lumps
of ice that break off
glaciers into the sea.

Mountains

DISCOVERY FACT™

Mount Everest is the highest mountain in the world.

Rain forest

DISCOVERY FACT™

More plants and animals
live in the rain forests than
any other place on Earth.

River

DISCOVERY FACT™

The longest river in the world is the River Nile in Egypt.

Volcano

DISCOVERY FACT™

Volcanoes have craters where lava and gas from beneath the Earth's crust burst through.

The deep pool at the bottom of a waterfall is called a "plunge pool."

Waterfall

Wave

DISCOVERY FACT™

The wind makes waves when it blows over the sea.

Lake

DISCOVERY FACT™

Lakes can be filled with fresh or salty water.

Storm

There are many different types of storm, including thunderstorms, snowstorms, and tornadoes.

Spring

In the spring, plants start to grow
and many animals are born.

Summer

DISCOVERY FACT™

The summer is the hottest season, when the sun shines the most.

In the fall, leaves turn red, brown, and yellow, and fall from the trees.

Fall

Winter

DISCOVERY FACT™

The winter is the coldest and darkest time of year.

Airport

DISCOVERY FACT™

Airports are where planes take off and land.

Plane

Planes are the fastest way to travel around the world.

Parks provide people in the city with green spaces to play sports and relax.

Park

Highway

Highways are long, straight roads that allow cars to go quickly between cities.

Ships

DISCOVERY FACT™

Ships carry passengers and goods all over the world.

Railroad

The railroad is a fast way
to travel over land.

Village

A village can be as big as a town, or have just a small number of houses.

DISCOVERY FACT™

More people live and work in cities than in the countryside.

City

Dam

DISCOVERY FACT™

Dams are used to make electricity from the power of moving water.

Earth

DISCOVERY FACT™

Earth is the only planet in our solar system where humans can live.

Moon

DISCOVERY FACT™

Only 1 side of the Moon can be seen from Earth.

Only 12 men have ever walked on the Moon.

Moon walk

Jupiter

Jupiter is the largest planet in our solar system.

Neptune

Neptune is the farthest planet from the Sun in our solar system.

Saturn's 9 rings are made from pieces of ice and rock.

Saturn

Shooting star

A shooting star is a piece of space rock that burns up as it falls to Earth.

Asteroid

DISCOVERY FACT™

Asteroids are lumps of rock and metal that orbit the Sun.

Telescope

DISCOVERY FACT™

Telescopes help
us see far
into space.

DISCOVERY FACT™

A launch pad is used to hold a rocket in place before blastoff.

Launch pad

Mission control

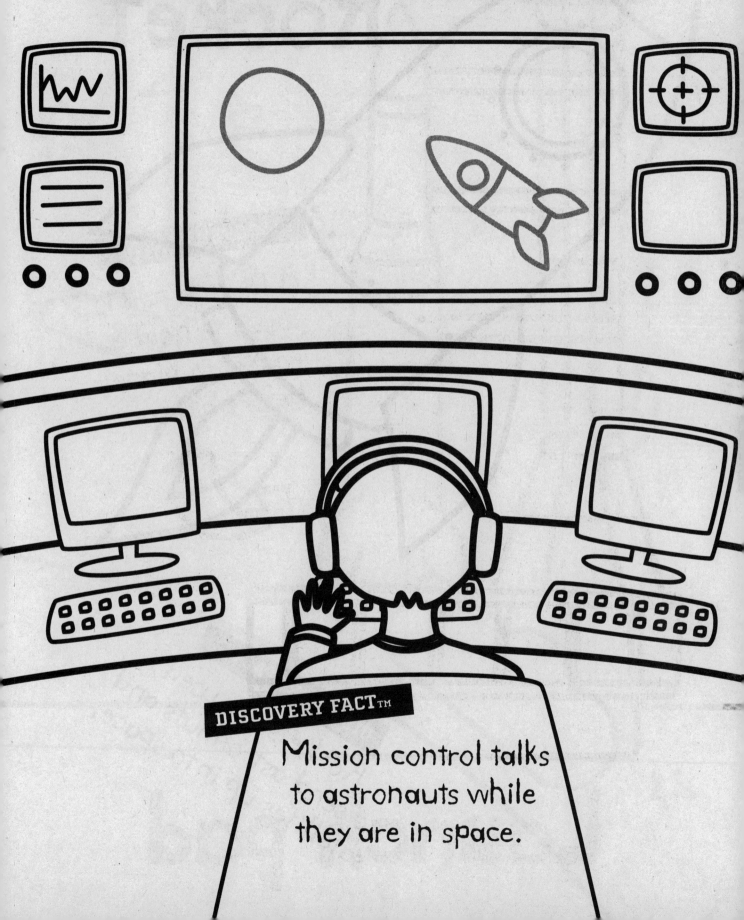

DISCOVERY FACT™

Mission control talks
to astronauts while
they are in space.

Rocket

DISCOVERY FACT™

Rockets are used to send astronauts and satellites up into space.

Astronauts are men and women who are trained to travel into space.

Astronaut

Space walk

DISCOVERY FACT™

A special spacesuit allows astronauts to breathe in space.

Satellites send TV images and telephone calls around the Earth.

Satellite

Space station

Seven astronauts can live on the space station at the same time.